Also by Mike Gipson:

Ocher's Dawn

Ocher's Rain

Ocher's Wind

Ocher's Fire

Fire

Ocher Jones Western Series

Book Four

Mike Gipson

This book is a work of fiction. Names, places and characters are the product of the author's imagination or are used fictitiously. Any resemblance to actual events or persons, living or dead, is coincidental.

Copyright © 2020 By Mike Gipson

Publisher – M.S. Gipson/KDP

ISBN-978-1-7321626-3-1

To

Gayle

*Through a half a century our fire
still burns brightly*

Acknowledgements

Anne Armezzani, Judy DeCarlo, Janet Schwick, Lourdes Schaffroth and Ann Vitale.

Thank You is not enough. But thank you for the time and effort you have given me in this endeavor.

Anne Armezzani – Book four, is it true? Only because you have pushed, pulled, and dragged me along the way.

Kacey, anything is possible as long as the fire still burns.

Characters –

Ocher Jones - Assassin, AKA Little Orphan, Traveler, named Shiilooshe by Ojos (Book 1), Ocher

Lewis & Amanda Livingston - Owners of the Double LL Ranch

Stacey Livingston - Daughter of Lewis & Amanda

Ollie Von Derr – Patron of the Von Derr clan. Two biological sons and eight adopted boys

Austin Peterson – accepted daughter of Monroe and Isabella Peterson.

Vernon Von Derr – one of Ollie's adopted boys

Holt Sturdevant – Texas Ranger

The Teacher and The Scorpion – Assassins.

Abel Jones – Frontiersman, friend who knows more than he should

And a few more.

Fire

Ocher's goal is simple. Peace. He knows that he is being hunted. Does he wait or eliminate the threat to himself and his goal? Is it his choice?
From a fire comes the pursuit, and a new life.

Chapter One

Fire! *It can be destructive, devastating, provide warmth or comfort and, in most cases, the opportunity to begin anew. From the ashes there can be new beginnings.*

"Where are the girls?" Ocher yells, as he jumps from the lead wagon.

"Upstairs, in the loft," screams Isabella Peterson as she runs toward the burning structure. She stops, turned back by the intense heat.

"How?" Ollie shouts, as he leaps from the second wagon.

"Three men rode up. They shot Monroe, set fire to the porch and rode off toward town," Isabella shrieks, making another attempt toward the house.

Ollie looks at the front of the small cabin fully engulfed in flames, the awning collapsing onto the porch itself, cutting off access to the front door.

"Is there a back way in?" Ocher shouts.

"No," Isabella replies between sobs.

"Ocher, get ready," Ollie says, as he calmly walks to the awning, grabs the flaming support beam with the palms of his hands and lifts it up. He bends slightly forward and with a guttural grunt lifts the load to his chest. Shifting his hands, he hoists the porch over his head.

Ocher needs no invitation. He runs through the front door, stepping over the body of Monroe Peterson. He can hear the wails of the girls in the loft.

As he climbs the ladder he hears Marta. "Ollie, your hands!" The sound of the awning hitting the ground follows.

Ocher quickly realizes that going back down the ladder and out the front door won't be possible.

There's only one place the girls can be. Ocher can hear their moans and follows the sound. Finally he sees their red hair, now black from the soot of the fire. Their freckled faces are covered in ash and streaked with tears.

Ocher looks at the underside of the roof. The shingles are nailed to the rafter beams with no visible nails in between. He's spent most of his life making his hands as hard as stone to be used as weapons. He sets his feet, clenches his fists and punches the shingle above his head. It gives. He continues his attack spurred on by the whimpering and coughing of the girls. His hands are swollen and bleeding but the shingles give and he can see daylight. He rips the adjoining shingles free. A hole.

"Come on, let's go," Ocher beckons to the girls.

Time is of the essence. Without hesitation, he grabs both girls and pushes Melissa up and out first. Next is Austin, then Ocher follows. The front of the house is in full flame. The back where they are standing will soon be engulfed. Ocher looks over the eave. It's about twenty feet to the ground. *I'll have to jump holding the girls. Better I break my legs than toss them off here.*

Ollie rounds the corner. His hands are burned to a bright red, his shirt and hair are streaming smoke. "I'll catch them, one at a time." He manages to get out between coughs.

Ocher grabs six year old Melissa, turns her to face him, gives her a kiss on the forehead and drops her toward Ollie. Before she can react to the fall, she's standing safely next to Marta. The adopted nine-year-old, Austin, sets her shoulders back, walks to the edge of the roof and jumps. Ocher looks down; both girls are safe.

Ollie looks up, "Jump."

Ocher hesitates, but jumps.

Ollie's level of exertion is no greater catching Ocher than it had been catching the girls. Ollie gasps for the third time, the contact hurting his burned hands.

Ollie and Ocher follow Marta back toward the front of the burning cabin. "I had to let go of the front porch. Figured you'd find a way out," Ollie remarks in between fits of coughing.

"We going to try and get Monroe's body out of there?" Ocher asks.

"Isabella said no. No use. She said he was dead before he hit the ground," Ollie finally gets through a complete sentence before starting to cough again.

Isabella is clutching the girls when Ollie and Ocher round the corner of the building.

Ollie's boys are sitting around the water trough on upturned buckets, each boy soaked to the skin.

"We couldn't stay ahead of the fire. Isabella said to stop," Marta says, as she carries a bucket of water toward the huddled Petersons.

Ocher walks over to Isabella, "The girls ok?"

She looks up, still too emotional to speak. Finally, she answers, "Thank you. All of you."

Ocher just nods not knowing what to say next.

In the distance, wagons, men on horseback, and Doc Simpson's buggy are hurrying toward the farm.

As the town folks arrive, they realize that fighting the fire is useless. They stand and gawk at the flames. Doc, with amazing agility, bounds from the buggy and heads straight for the girls still huddled in Isabella's arms.

The Doc makes a quick visual assessment of the girls, Ollie and Ocher. "Boys, bring me three buckets of clean fresh water."

Ollie's boys scramble to fulfill the Doctor's orders.

"Ollie, put your hands in that water. It'll help draw out some of the heat. Ocher, you do the same. It will help keep the swelling down. I'll tend to you both as soon as I can."

Doc Simpson overturns a bucket, sits down, drags the third bucket of water to his side. He beckons Melissa over to him. "You hurt anywhere, Melissa?"

"No," she whispers.

He reaches into his vest pocket and pulls out a handkerchief, wets it and wipes the soot from her face. "Still pretty as ever. You sure nothing hurts?"

"Yes."

Austin, being Austin, walks over to the clean water bucket and pretty much sticks her whole head in it. She stands and throws her head back flinging water everywhere. "I ain't hurt, Doc. Just in my heart. I'll miss PaPa, a lot."

"We all will, Austin. He was a good man." Doc stands and walks over to a short, well dressed man. "Harold, you got some rooms for these folks? Be a good idea to get them away from all of this."

Harold Willard, owner of the Prairie Inn, replies, "Sure, Doc. I'll get them into town right away."

Doc then pivots and starts toward Ollie. "Let's see them hands."

Ollie holds up his hands, the water dripping back into the bucket.

Marta gasps from behind the Doc.

"Marta, see that yellow green plant out there beyond the corral?"

"Yes."

"That's Yellow-Spined Thistle. Have the boys gather a batch of the blossoms and bring it here."

"I want to help," says Austin.

Before Marta can tell the boys what she wants, Austin has the boys gathering the blossoms.

"When they get back, mash up the blossoms and make a paste and apply it to his hands," the Doc says, as he demonstrates mashing a blossom between his palms.

Marta nods. Austin arrives having confiscated all of the blossoms from the boys. Marta accepts a handful of the blossoms and reduces them into a paste between her palms.

"Ollie, those hands are going to hurt like all get out for a while. The salve will help. Now Ocher, let's see your hands," the Doctor orders.

Ocher pulls his hands out of the water and holds them out for Doc to see.

"What did you do that caused this?" Doc Simpson says, holding Ocher right hand to examine it.

"He punched his way through the roof to get the girls out," Ollie offers, knowing Ocher won't tell the tale.

"With your fists? You punched a hole?" Doc asks, looking at Ocher.

"Yep."

"I'd say not possible, but here we are. Nothing broke that I can tell. Get some Witch Hazel to put on those knuckles. It'll help with the swelling. For now keep them hands in that cold water for a bit."

"Ok. Thanks, Doc."

Ollie looks over at Ocher, "I've seen that look too many times. What's on your mind?"

"Why? Simple as that. Why?" Ocher replies.

Ollie stands, leans back against a corral rail as Marta applies medicine. "A diversion?" she offers.

"Looks like we got more company headed our way," Ollie says, wincing as Marta applies the salve.

"From two directions," Ocher says, pointing with his dripping left hand.

Lewis, Amanda and Stacey gallop into the yard. Stacey comes toward Ocher, Amanda toward Isabella with Lewis taking care of the horses.

"Isabella, if you..." Amanda starts.

"Thank you, Amanda, but right now we need to care for the girls and them," she says, pointing her chin toward Ollie and Ocher. "Grieving will come, in time."

"Let me see, Ocher," Stacey demands.

Ocher holds out his wet, dripping hands.

"Yours too," she says to Ollie.

He holds out his hands now covered in ointment.

"Marta, can't we leave these two alone for a moment?"

"Good thing they were here. We'd have lost the girls in addition to Monroe," Marta answers, as she tries to finish her application of ointment to Ollie's hands.

Stacey looks at Ocher then Ollie, "Oh no, Monroe is dead? I'll be back." Stacey turns and strides toward the crowd gathered around Isabella and the girls.

"That looks like the sheriff headed this way in a big hurry," Ollie says, pointing with his chin.

"The way he's hard riding that horse he can't be headed here to help," Ocher responds, as he stands to intercept the sheriff.

"The bank, three men robbed the bank," the sheriff yells as he dismounts.

Ocher turns to Marta and Ollie, "Yep. Marta, you were right. A diversion."

Chapter Two

The family has gathered for supper under the oversized awning that Marta calls her summer kitchen. "Too many of us to sit inside. It'll be better in the summer kitchen."

The Livingstons, the hands of the Double LL, Ollie, Marta and the eight boys, Ocher, Bug and now the Petersons. *The Family* .

The amount of food on the table reflects what a small army would require. In fact, it is a small army.

At the far end of the table, Austin's overseeing the boys, especially Vernon.

Ocher has given up trying to manipulate his knife and fork, choosing to feed on hand-held food. His hands are still too swollen.

"You leaving in the morning, Ocher?" Ollie asks. The pain in Ollie's face reflects the effort of trying to hold onto food, or anything else. His recovery will take a bit of time.

"Yep. Tracking them won't be too hard. If it's the three men I think it is, they'll leave a trail. With an estimated fifty thousand dollars, well, they'll spend it like it was water."

"That's a lot of good people's money. Sure will hurt a lot of folks if they get away with it," Lewis remarks, as he looks up at the rider coming in.

"Ocher, got some news for you," Sheriff Henry Thaddeus, says. "And an offer."

"Ok, Henry, what's the news?"

"Your friend Holt has been deputized as a United States Marshall. He's headed here. He telegraphed to say you get started and he'll follow your trail and catch up."

"Ok. What's the offer?" Ocher asks.

"I have been authorized to deputize you as well, if you want."

Ocher takes a drink of coffee and sets down the cup. "No. I don't want to be constrained by the law. I don't plan on becoming a vigilante, but those boys stepped way outside decency when they went after the Petersons. Need be, well if need be... let's let it go at that, Henry."

"Thought that would be what you'd say. Just in case, here's a Marshall's badge," the sheriff says, laying a badge on the table. "Keep account of your necessities. You'll get them paid for. Good luck."

Chapter Three

During the heated discussion earlier with the sheriff, Ocher's argued, "A following posse will put up a dust cloud and be visible. One rider shouldn't be visible, if he's careful." Ocher wins out.

The mid-October morning is just beginning over Ocher's right shoulder as he crosses the trail of three horses, with no pack animals, riding hard. *This bunch hasn't put much thought into the escape.*

"Well, horse, too early to tell where they're headed. Could be Santa Fe, or maybe Las Vegas, New Mexico."

The Pinto doesn't respond.

"They could have a rendezvous planned somewhere up ahead or an ambush, but not likely. They don't strike me as being that smart."

The Pinto whinnies at that statement.

The day is warm but not the typical hot of Texas and the trail's clear and straight. Ocher stops at noon for coffee and a biscuit, also to rest the horses. The group ahead will soon have to stop or walk. The horses are being ridden too hard. There's been no indication of a night camp or even a cold camp for a rest. Their horses will soon give out, and it's beginning to look like no rendezvous was planned. The thieves thought there'd be no one in pursuit.

As the sun fades, and Ocher moves further north, the sunset carries a chill. Cold isn't something Ocher's ever experienced. He's been chilled before, but never cold. He'll have to get appropriate clothing to help him cope with the new experience if the three head into the mountains.

The Rio Hondo is another three or four hours ride and Ocher knows that the horses ahead can't go further than the river. He doesn't want to ride into the three, so he stops well short of the river for the night. He camps below a rise, keeping a foothill between his camp and where he suspects the bank robbers have stopped.

Just at sundown a flash of light from his back trail gets his full attention. Someone is trailing him. *If that's the sheriff, well, I'll send him packing.*

Ocher takes out his spy glass and focuses in on the rider. *Can't be, but sure looks like. Vernon.*

Ocher smiles and just shakes his head. He waits for the boy to ride into camp.

Vernon can see Ocher above the camp as he dismounts.

Ocher puts his finger across his lips telling Vernon to be quiet and then beckons him to come up the hill.

"We'll talk this over in a bit, Vernon. For now you sit tight. I'll be right back," Ocher whispers.

Vernon nods.

Ocher climbs the hill with great care and looks over the river valley before him. There isn't any sign of fire, camp or other activity. Using his telescope he searches the valley below. There's no activity. He walks back to Vernon.

"Let's go, Vernon," Ocher says, as he walks past the boy.

"We gonna camp here tonight?"

"No, Vernon. Right now we're going to find Austin."

"Austin? I don't understand."

"I don't understand either. But I know she's probably trailing you."

"She wouldn't come out here alone. She's only a girl," Vernon says defensively.

"Vernon, there ain't no such thing as just a girl. Get in the saddle. Let's go."

The Pinto doesn't fuss when Ocher throws on the saddle blanket and steps up into the stirrup. "All right, horse. Go find her."

It doesn't take long. The Pinto seems to know right where to go. The moon's just risen when the Pinto stops and points his ears. Just off the trail Ocher can hear a horse whinny. "Stay here, Vernon."

Ocher steps down and leads the Pinto in the direction the horse has alerted. Austin's standing next to her horse, trying to keep it quiet.

"Austin, it's me, Ocher. You ok?"

"Yes. Didn't know who was coming in. Lost Vernon's trail. Was going to watch for a camp fire then sneak up to see who was there."

"Good thinking. He's with me. Vernon, come on in. What say we set up camp here and talk this over?"

"I'm hungry. Can we eat?" Austin asks.

"No need for a cold camp. We'll get a fire going and eat. Did either of you bring any supplies?"

"Of course," replies Austin. "I don't know about him," she says, pointing at Vernon.

"I have supplies. I ain't no tenderfoot," Vernon retorts.

"Enough. You two came trailing me wanting to be treated as grown-ups. The men we're trailing, well, you seen what they did. Right now we have to all be grown-ups."

Both nod. "Yes, Uncle Ocher," Vernon says.

"Ok. Someone gather firewood and plenty of it. I'll get a lean-to constructed to hold in the heat. There's bacon and biscuits in the kit on the saddle pack horse. And the horses need to be fed and picketed. Any questions?"

"No, Uncle Ocher," Austin says smiling.

Ocher smiles, "Good."

The colder it gets, the closer the three move toward the fire. "I heard from a Crow Indian friend of mine that white men build a big fire and move away. An Indian makes a small fire and sits close in," Ocher says, starting the conversation.

"We must be both," Austin says. "We got a big fire and we're sitting pretty close."

"Uncle Ocher, you mad at us?" Vernon asks.

Ocher hesitates, finally, "Being mad won't get us anywhere. I suspect sending you back won't accomplish anything. You'll just try it again."

Both nod.

"You'll have to do as I say. Exactly what I say. Understand?"

"Yes, Uncle Ocher," comes from both.

"Ok. No need for a night watch. At least not tonight. The horses will alert us if anybody gets close. Let's get some rest."

Chapter Four

The chill wakes him well before dawn. The swelling in his hands, from his confrontation with roof shingles, has gone down. Austin is snuggled up close to him on one side and Vernon on the other.

He snakes out into the inhospitable morning. It's an effort to build a small fire and make coffee. He's never been this cold, not even after swimming ashore with Ojos, when they jumped overboard on his trip to America. His fingers are drawn and pale. He can see his breath and his boots seem larger. He decides that winter will not be his favorite season. The Pinto and the mule fuss about, apparently not pleased with the temperature either. They settle down while being saddled, anxious to get moving in the pre-dawn.

Austin sits up and comments, "The sun ain't even up yet." Realizing her mistake, she continues, "Time to get on the trail."

"Yep, hit the trail," Vernon echoes.

"We have time for coffee," Ocher says, "then hit the trail."

The three reach the Rio Hondo just at dawn. They search but can't discover a cold camp or any indication that the fleeing gang paused even for a rest. Instead of stopping, they forded the river and kept going.

"Come here, you two," Ocher beckons them over. "See the sign the men are leaving? The horses are in rough condition. They're all done in. The hoof prints are elongated, showing that the horses are not stepping up but dragging their feet."

Vernon leans down and traces the hoof mark with his finger.

"The trail coming out of the river is even more revealing. The prints show that the horses are struggling. Where there should be a clean hoof print of a sure-footed horse, each print shows multiple prints." Ocher continues with the lesson. "The horses are so tired that they can't gain purchase on the slight incline of the river bank."

They continue following the trail. An hour later they find the first dead horse. The fleeing men are now down to two horses and three riders. They'll have to steal or buy horses or stop. At least they put the horse down before moving on.

Ocher lets the two youngsters take the lead following the sign. The trail is easy to follow. What normally would be a straight line, or close to it, meanders as the horses struggle with each step.

As they top a ridge, both Austin and Vernon pull up.

"There's a ranch down there," Vernon turns and tells Ocher.

Ocher rides up alongside. He sits silently for a moment, "Ok you two. Read the sign."

The ranch is down on the flat of an east west valley.

Austin is first to comment, "Looks like a working ranch, but no smoke coming from the chimney or the bunk house."

"Ain't no hands milling about doing ranch work. Just two horses in the corral," Vernon adds.

"Good, you two. Very good. Now the hard part. Stay here. I'm going to check the house. If I come out without my hat, you two high tail it northwest of here to Alhambra, but leave the Pinto. If I come out with my hat on, it's all right to come down. Ok?"

"Yes, Uncle Ocher," in unison.

Very cautiously he approaches from behind the main house. Everything appears too quiet. There's no movement in the house or surrounding barn or corrals. He fears the worst. He works his way around the small log building, stopping at each window to peer in. All the curtains are pulled shut and there's no light from the interior. Finally he stops, reaches the front, back tracks to the corner of the porch. Standing in front of the door could invite trouble.

"Hello in the house." No answer and no movement. He repeats the hail and gets the same result. Ocher cautiously approaches the front entrance, pauses, listens and opens the door.

There are two people in the room, both have been beaten. The woman opens one swollen eye and closes it quickly. "We're friendly," Ocher says to the woman playing possum.

She struggles to sit up, wide-eyed and scared. "See to Clovis," she motions toward the man.

Ocher moves to check Clovis. "Got a strong pulse," Ocher stands and walks to the door. He walks out far enough for Austin and Vernon to see him.

It's frigid in the room, as the fire in the fireplace has gone out some time ago. Clovis comes around. Both Clovis and Elizabeth Narvone are mad, thirsty, hungry, and cold but mostly mad.

Austin and Vernon enter the cabin. "One of you get a fire going. We need to get some water on to boil to clean up those wounds. Need to get some coffee going too. Got to get these folks warmed up."

There's no argument. Austin grabs a bucket and heads to the well for water and Vernon grabs some kindling and wood to start a fire.

Ocher starts to clean Clovis' face with a wet rag but Elizabeth steps over, "I'll do that if you can get some bacon going."

Austin sides up against Elizabeth, "Ma'am let me clean you up. Uncle Ocher can take care of your man."

"I'll get the bacon going," Vernon chimes in.

Clovis winches as Ocher dabs blood from the man's cheek, "'Bout midnight three men broke into the house and just beat us. It appears," Clovis continues after looking around the room, "they took what they wanted from in here."

"They rode in on two worn out horses. I'd guess they took whatever stock they needed. We'll check the barn and corral in a bit," Ocher says, as he wrings out the cloth in the bowl being shared with Austin.

Vernon walks over with a coffee pot and cups and starts to pour. "Bacon will be ready in a bit."

"There was some fresh baked bread in that cupboard over there," Elizabeth says. "If they didn't take it."

After some camp medicine, coffee, bacon and fresh bread, Ocher and Clovis walk to the barn to confirm the theft of three horses and two pack mules. The two horses they left are in bad shape and probably will have to be put down. The rest of the stock had been turned out but are returning to the barn to be fed.

"Only caught part of their palavering," Clovis recounts. "Sounded like they was headed to Fort Collins, Colorado, Salt Lake City then to California." He rubs his chin, "Mighty ambitious to even consider crossing the mountains from Fort Collins to Salt Lake this time of year. The snow and cold have no mercy and these three sure don't appear to be trail smart. Just look at the horses they rode in. These three are riding right into trouble."

Elizabeth insists that they stay for dinner before continuing the chase. "As dumb as they appear to be, they'll drunk up in some town for a day or two."

Elizabeth shows Austin and Vernon the finer art of wringing a chicken's neck and plucking it before cooking. The three intruders have outfitted themselves out of her kitchen and pantry, but she still sets out a glorious meal.

Over the meal, Clovis passes on every piece of trail knowledge he can: short cuts, bogs, quick sand, hide outs, including people and places to avoid. The meal is great but the information is even better.

"Ocher, here's a letter of introduction, if needed. The spreads you'll be riding through have good ranchers. Just in case those yahoos you're chasing have muddied the water. You can send a telegram in Alhambra to those kids' folks." Clovis looks at Austin and Vernon. "Good young uns, real good."

"Thanks, Clovis."

With three or so hours left before sunset Ocher heads north to get to Alhambra to send a message.

The Pinto complains slightly about the extra weight Ocher has put on at Elizabeth's table but heads out snorting and rested.

Chapter Five

At Alhambra Ocher sends a telegram:

Austin and Vernon are safe and with me.
We will continue the chase. Not to worry.

At the Alhambra Dry Goods Emporia, Ocher manages to wrangle Vernon into trying on cold weather clothing while doing the same with Austin. In addition, Austin is outfitted as a cow hand. No use advertising that she's a lady in the making. As a bribe, Ocher buys some rock candy, just to get them to stand still long enough to get outfitted.

The moon's full so they decide to ride on and camp after a few hours. "We'll make a cold camp for tonight. Still mighty close to town," Ocher advises, as they unsaddle and picket the horses. "We'll have a fire in the morning to warm up and for coffee."

Both Austin and Vernon nod their weary heads. The sugar in the candy is finally wearing off.

During the following day, Ocher and his sidekicks make two quick stops at ranches, one at Vaughn the other at Dillia. They're greeted as friends at both. Ocher takes the time to pick up more trail knowledge. The hands at both ranches have seen signs of the passing trio. In one instance, the bandits had butchered a steer, taking enough for a meal and leaving the rest to rot. All signs indicate they're moving straight toward Fort Collins.

In the late afternoon, Ocher can feel and hear something pelting his sombrero. He holds out his hand up and sees white pellets gathering in his palm.

"That's sleet, Uncle Ocher," Austin offers, as she rides up alongside him.

"We best find shelter and get a fire going while we have daylight," Ocher says, as Vernon rides up on the opposite side from Austin.

They find shelter in a hollowed out cliff face that provides a break from the wind and sleet. The horses are picketed in a copse of evergreens providing them a little shelter.

After gathering wood and getting the fire started, Ocher declares, "Might as well cook us a proper meal. Make the best of it."

A hind quarter of venison is roasting over the fire, skillet bread is baking, coffee is ready and the three are hungry. He's just about to cut off a slice of the venison when the Pinto's ears go up. Ocher calmly moves away from the fire and into the shadows with his Spencer.

There are two riders, Indians, a young brave and an elder warrior. They present no threat. They don't step down but show their empty hands in his direction. Ocher steps out so he can be seen, then points toward the fire and the food, "Welcome."

The elder warrior nods and dismounts.

Ocher points again toward the grove of trees, "Horses there."

The young brave takes the horses off to where the Pinto is and hobbles the ponies.

Communications are difficult but Ocher learns that the older man is a Sioux Chief, Red Bluff, and the younger Indian is his son, Standing Bear. The two are headed to Fort Collins to a treaty signing. They're representing their clan at the signing. They've dropped down out of the foothills because of the weather.

Red Bluff points to the Squash Blossom Conch that Ocher is wearing, "Apache?"

"Yes. White Elk," Ocher responds.

Red Bluff just grunts at the explanation.

They eat, talk, and settle in for the evening, accepting each other's company.

The sleet and wind subside during the night and morning is bright, beautiful and cold.

After a breakfast of bread and venison, Red Bluff and Standing Bear gather their gear and walk to the horses. They lead the ponies back to the campsite. Before mounting his barebacked pony, Red Bluff points to the conch Ocher is wearing, "White Elk, brave enemy," and rides away.

Chapter Six

Ocher, Austin and Vernon arrive in Las Vegas Wells on the seventeenth day, around three in the afternoon. He goes directly to the telegraph office, sends a message, and then goes to the Sheriff's office.

"Yep, they was through here, left yesterday about sunup. They acted like a bunch of yearlings, flashed around money, and paid no attention to their mounts. By now every low life in the territory knows they got money. Trouble, courting trouble for sure. Made no secret about it. They was headed to Fort Collins to see the goings on."

Ocher gets a description of the three men and immediately confirms who they are. "I had a run in with these three in San Antonio, and in El Paso. A Texas Ranger friend of mine said they were headed for trouble." Ocher thanks the sheriff and returns to the telegraph office. Austin and Vernon were left at the store to gather supplies and sample the hard candy.

A reply to Ocher's telegram is waiting when he returns to the Telegraph Office:

(1) $52,421.85 was stolen from the bank.
(2) Holt and company in Alhambra
    awaiting instructions.

Ocher sends two telegrams. One goes to Pine Springs, the other to Alhambra. Both messages are the same:

Headed to Fort Collins.
Traveling companions fine.

A reply from Alhambra is immediate:

Meet you there.

Ocher wonders about *and company* deciding it probably is another marshal. Not something he wants to exchange telegrams over.

His traveling companions have the supplies already packed when Ocher arrives back at the store. Both have what looks like a large chaw of tobacco pooched out one side of a cheek.

"Jawbreaker," Vernon mumbles around the mass. At least that's what Ocher thinks he says.

Austin holds out what looks like a big round red rock in her hand, "Got you one if you want it."

Ocher accepts the challenge. Now all three are sitting on the front porch with puffed out cheeks.

"Holt and another marshal are meeting us in Fort Collins. The bank robbers are about a day or so ahead of us," Ocher says around his jawbreaker. "You two ready?"

Both nod, more interested in the candy than the conversation.

The trail's easy to follow. Even a day or so old, it's plain as can be. The three men are now taking the ride a bit easier.

"They don't seem to be hiding their trail," Vernon observes.

"They don't think they're being followed," Ocher answers.

"Bad mistake," Austin adds.

One day, the normally straight trail takes a deviation.

"Looks like they're avoiding the mountains and Denver by setting trail a little further east," Ocher says, as he stands after looking at the hoof prints left on the trail. "They'll skirt the foothills. Won't be as cold. Could be headed toward Fort Collins."

Little by little the three pursuers close the distance. At Gilchrist the last outpost before Fort Collins, they come in at noon.

Gilchrist has no sheriff, just a man at the stable and a clerk/bartender acting as the town gossip. "Yep, they was here, those three. Left 'bout sunrise."

They move on quickly although they've been on the trail three weeks. Today is the day they'll catch the robbers.

Chapter Seven

"See that ridge up there?" Ocher points up the mountain to their west. "We're going up there, have a cold camp and look around."

"No coffee?" Austin remarks.

"Nope. Don't want to alert those three we're following or anybody else that might be trailing them. So, no coffee."

They ride behind the ridge, "You two take care of the horses and get something to eat. I'll be right back," Ocher says, as he starts up the ridge.

At the peak of the ridge, Ocher takes his spyglass and methodically checks the valley. He slides back below the ridge to where Austin and Vernon are waiting. Austin hands Ocher a biscuit.

"The three we're after are at the head of this valley north of us," Ocher starts his report.

"You say that like there are more riders out there," Austin observes.

"Yep. There are four men riding hard from the east headed right for the other three. There's nothing we can do against seven men. It doesn't matter whether they're together or not. We'll just have to sit tight and see what happens. I got a bad feeling about those four. You two stay here and be ready to ride. I'm going back up on the ridge."

There's no reply from the two, just nods.

Ocher can see and hear the execution. He can't stop it. The four men ride directly into the camp, open up with a barrage of gunfire and execute the three bank robbers. Ocher's only thought is: *they didn't really care if those men were the ones with the money or not. They didn't care.*

The three dead men are stripped of their gear, tied behind the stolen horses and the horses stampeded into the high desert plains. The remainder of the gear is dumped into a ravine, the men taking only the saddle bags containing the bank's money.

Ocher stays on the ridge just long enough to watch the four men take up residence in the bank robbers' camp. He works his way back down the ridge to Austin and Vernon.

"We heard gun fire," Vernon says.

"Yep. Those four coming from the east rode right in and shot the other three," Ocher answers.

"How did they know that those were the men that robbed the bank?" Austin asks.

"Don't know. They didn't seem to care. That's the kind of men we're now dealing with.

You two have been good traveling companions. Now it's different. You two have to stay put while I do...well what I've got to do. Understand?"

There's no reply.

It is indeed a cold camp. The three huddle up for the night, but don't sleep much.

"I'm going to ride up a little higher and come down to that other camp from the west. That way they won't think I'm trailing them. You two wait here until the sun gets to about midway up to noon. Here's my spyglass," Ocher hands his telescope to Vernon.

"Watch for me to come into their camp. If things go wrong, you two head south to Gilcrest."

"Yes, Uncle Ocher," both Austin and Vernon respond not knowing enough to be afraid or reassured.

"I won't be there long. Just for a cup of coffee then I'll ride out. Just keep watch. I won't be going far. When I ride back into their camp and things go as I plan, I'll wave my hat and you two can come on down. Understand?"

They both nod.

"Ok. Austin repeat what I just said."

Austin repeats the plan.

"Now you, Vernon."

He does the same.

"Any questions?"

Both shake their heads. There are none.

Moving to a different location, Ocher also makes camp, a cold camp, and it is cold. He huddles in the oversized clothes that he bought and makes a plan. He doesn't want to let the money get any further away, but he doesn't want to just kill these men although he has the capability but no longer the inclination for it.

Ocher rides to the west before turning east thinking about his plan. His Yaqui Indian friend, Manny, has provided a solution to subdue the four men. Ocher just has to pull it off.

"Hello in camp."

"Come on in," comes the reply.

Ocher rides in with the Sharpes across the saddle aimed in the general direction of the men. After being invited he dismounts, "Coffee smells mighty good. Mind if I pour me some?"

The oldest of the four men watches Ocher warily and finally says, "Help yourself."

Ocher, in one smooth movement, pours a cup of coffee and drops a small pouch into the enameled pot. The pouch contains a mixture of desert flowers, herbs and roots that are used by the Yaqui Indian Medicine People to render the injured unconscious while being tended to. With luck, these four will be drugged when they drink their coffee. Ocher just sets the coffee pot back close to the fire and sits on his haunches.

"You headed to the big doings up to the Fort?" the older man asks.

"Yep, thought I'd ride up, before I head on southwest for the winter. Maybe I'll see you there. Burning daylight. Thanks for the coffee."

Ocher moves to the Pinto, mounts and moves quickly out of range before any of the four can make a move. These are four very dangerous men, and he doesn't want to give them any opportunity to corner him. He rides north about half an hour then circles back south of the camp. The four men have finished the coffee. Although they aren't unconscious, they are drugged, disoriented and will be manageable, long enough for Ocher to get the four to Fort Collins.

He steps to the edge of the camp and waves his hat, signaling his two companions.

Chapter Eight

"Uncle Ocher, is this the way cowboys live?" Austin asks. "I mean, well, we been on the trail what seems like forever. It ain't an adventure no more."

"I don't know much about the cowboy way, Austin. I agree living from camp fire to camp fire can get a person weary," Ocher responds, turning in the saddle to check on the four drugged men.

"Even Vernon ain't talking 'bout being a cowboy no more," Austin continues.

"Well, cowboy, we got one more hard ride before we'll get to Fort Collins. Then we can all step out of the saddle," Ocher says. "How about you ride drag for a bit and let Vernon come up?"

"Ok, Uncle Ocher."

The ride to Fort Collins takes all day and all night. The only stops are for *coffee*. The four men stay in the saddle out of habit, but have no idea where they are or where they're going.

The caravan arrives in town just at sunrise. The Fort consists of two sections: the civilian

town and the Army fort. Ocher rides directly to
the Sheriff's Office in the civilian section.

"Vernon, go in and see if the sheriff is
there."

"Morning, boy. You look plumb worn out,"
the man behind the desk observes.

"Yes, sir. You the sheriff?" Vernon inquires.

"I am."

"We have some bad men outside. Could you
come out and talk to my uncle?"

The big, well-traveled man with searching
eyes follows Vernon outside. The sheriff looks
past Ocher at the four men still on horseback.
He readjusts his focus back to Ocher, "George
Walsenburg, Sheriff of this territory. I'm real
interested in how you come to have that
McCaskle bunch so tame."

"Ocher, Sheriff. Perhaps we should lock
them up before they change their attitude."

Ocher and the Sheriff, with Austin and
Vernon following, escort the four men into the
cell area, lock them in and come back into the
office. There's coffee on the small pot-bellied
stove and Ocher pours himself a cup, after it's
offered.

Austin takes the saddlebags from her
shoulder and drops them onto the desk.

"I haven't looked into those saddle bags but
when they left the bank in Pine Springs, Texas
they contained $52,421.85. Those four murdered
the three men who robbed the bank back in mid-

October. We've been on the trail since then. A U.S. Marshal is trailing behind."

The Sheriff sits silently, takes a sip of coffee. "OK, no doubt that those four did what you say, but I'll hold the saddle bags 'til the marshal gets here. What did you do to McCaskle and the other three? I've never seen men in that condition."

Ocher takes the time to tell the Sheriff the whole story.

"Well, Ocher, you are a very ingenious man. By the way, there's a reward for that bunch, and I'll get the paperwork going on that." He looks over at the two youngsters. "You two look done in."

Both Austin and Vernon nod. After three weeks they are too cowboyed out to talk.

"Now, as you can see, there's a big ta-doo here 'bouts with the signing of the Indian Treaty in ten days. There are people coming in from everywhere to see the Indians, the Eastern big wigs, the signing, and the spectacle of the whole shin dig. There ain't a room to be had anywhere, and a cowboy can't afford to eat but once a week at these prices."

"We'll find some place to set up camp until the marshal gets here," Ocher says.

"I can do better. East of here, I have a small cabin I use, when I have a chance to hunt and fish. You can use that if you want. Most of the lookers are camping out within a mile or so of the Fort. The cabin is out about five miles, so you shouldn't have to be bothered by all of this, unless you want to be."

"Thanks, we'll take you up on that," Ocher replies.

Both Austin and Vernon nod their approval.

"When the marshal shows up, I'll send him along."

While giving Ocher directions to the cabin, the Sheriff methodically counts the money in the saddlebags and gives Ocher a receipt for fifty-two thousand dollars.

"Thanks again. By the way, when the potion wears off that bunch, they're going to be in a mighty foul mood. They won't remember much, but they'll be ornery for a day or so."

Turning to his traveling companions, "I believe we've earned a decent meal. What say we find a place to eat and have a real breakfast?"

"Can I have some hot cakes?" Austin asks.

"Me too?" Vernon echoes.

"That sounds mighty good. After that we can stock up on some supplies and go out to the cabin and hunker down."

The Sheriff is right about the prices, but they need some coffee, beans, bacon and sundries. After restocking their supplies, including three jawbreakers, they ride out.

Chapter Nine

The whole troop is exhausted as they arrive at the cabin. The saving grace in the extra effort is they're away from the people crowded into the Fort area. They arrive at the cabin just as the sun sets.

"Nice looking cabin," Vernon notes.

"There's even a corral for the horses," Austin adds.

"Well, let's unpack, take care of the horses, fix supper and well...I think that will be enough," Ocher says, stepping down from the Pinto.

Ocher rubs down the horses, feeds them, then turns them loose in the corral. He returns to the cabin following the odor of biscuits and beans.

Ocher is cleaning up supper dishes. "We'll look around in the morning." It's too late. Austin and Vernon are asleep in the bunk beds. He grabs his bedroll, stokes the fire and calls it a day.

Early the next morning, Austin and Vernon don't even complain about having cold biscuits for breakfast. They just want to go exploring. After stoking the fire, the three head out the door.

The cabin sits well back of the trail hidden from any casual look. A mountain meadow is visible to the west and a snow fed spring to the east, with several pools of clear water.

"Man-oh-man, look at those trout. How about trout for supper, Uncle Ocher?" Vernon says, pointing at the clear water.

"You two can go fishing. I'm going to heat some water and take a bath," Austin declares.

"We can all use some cleaning. Along with our clothes. We'll take turns, fishing and cleaning. Ok?"

"Fishing first," Vernon declares, heading off to cut a limb for a pole.

"Boys..." is all Austin says, as she turns and heads toward the cabin.

By day's end the three have bathed, some quicker than others, clothes have been washed and dried. The trout fried with wild onions, garlic and potatoes is perfect after three weeks on the trail. Firewood has been gathered and stacked to maintain the fire in the cabin. As before, Ocher is just finishing dishes when he can hear Austin snoring from the top bunk.

The weather turns colder and Ocher has his first experience with snow. The flurry doesn't last long but long enough for Ocher to realize what an impact a large volume of snow could create.

For the next eight days Ocher takes the opportunity to teach his traveling companions some skills.

Ocher makes each of the two a rock sling. Austin's first effort almost results in taking out the only window in the cabin. Vernon's isn't much better. After a lot of practice they both can hit what they aim at.

Ocher also teaches them some of his special skills. Mainly how to escape from being held, just in case.

The camp hums along. Hunting, fishing cleaning and resting. The three take short rides during a couple of the days at the beginning of their stay, but even this far from the Fort the amount of humanity moving toward the treaty signing is visible.

Around sunset on the eight day, they hear, "Hello in the cabin."

Ocher recognizes the voice. It's Holt.

As Ocher steps through the door he sees the other rider. So do Austin and Vernon.

"Miss Stacey," Austin declares, running past Ocher.

Holt just looks at Ocher, "Think you could have stopped her?"

"Not likely," Ocher answers, smiling at Stacey.

Stacey steps down, swoops up Austin for a hug, puts her down and walks casually toward Ocher, "Hello cowboy."

The hug Austin just received isn't like the hug Ocher receives.

"I'm glad you're here," Ocher whispers in her ear.

Finally Ocher lets go of Stacey, "You two go on in. We'll take care of the horses."

Austin grabs the reins of Stacey's horse, Vernon, Holt's horse, leaving Ocher to unload the pack horse. His two companions are finished and in the cabin long before he finishes.

Ocher arrives back at the cabin just as another flurry begins, a lot heavier than before.

Holt is standing beside the stove, biscuit in hand, coffee not far away, "There are more folks in Fort Collins than I've seen in all of Texas. Man can't even spit. A lot of fuss for just signing a piece of paper. If it's Indians those folks want to see, they just need to ride across the Arizona Territory. They'll meet all the Indians they can handle." Holt has spoken more in one minute than all the time Ocher had known him.

"Almost as bad as New York," Stacey adds.

"I take it, you two are ready to head back to Texas," Ocher smiles as he speaks.

"Need a couple days to rest up. We'll be ready," Holt answers. "We stopped by the sheriff's office coming through town. That's how we found you. We know he's got the bank money, too,"

Stacey adds. "I'm ready."

"Sounds fine, I'd like to stop by a small outfit just north of Arabela on the way and check on a couple of folks. Be good for a sit down meal anyway. Elizabeth sets a mighty fine table."

"Ocher, sounds to me like you're going to eat your way through the West." They all laugh as the snow flurry continues.

The next day is a day for repacking the outfits on Holt's pack mule, deciding on supplies, resting both men, women, kids and horses. Austin brings down a turkey with her rock sling and cooks up the bird for supper along with some wild vegetables. Stacey makes a rough berry cobbler made from blueberries brought from home in a jar.

They leave for Fort Collins rested and ready for the trip home to Texas, arriving just after sunrise at the Sheriff's Office. George is pleased to see the troop and turn over the saddlebags with the bank's money.

"Mighty glad to get rid of those saddlebags, I don't envy you traveling with that all the way back to Texas. I wouldn't mind getting out of here for a while, just to get away from all of these people, but not with those saddlebags. I put fifteen hundred more in there for the reward for the McCaskle's. Good thing you're leaving. It might take that much just to eat for a day or two around here. Good luck to you."

"Thanks, Sheriff. Next time you're in Pine Creek, stop by my ranch. You'll be welcome anytime," Ocher says as he picks up the saddlebags and heads for the door. Within half an hour the column moves out of town toward home.

Chapter Ten

The smallest things can spark a memory, a warning or create dread. It's just a smell that invokes all of these emotions at once.

Ocher is first. Stacey tries not to react but her back straightens and she goes all most rigid. Finally Holt.

"Just keep riding," Ocher cautions.

He wants to look for the source of the smell but knows better. He can't give anything away. He also knows he can't just ride away. *There's an assassin here, probably two. Who are the assassins here to kill, me or someone else? Just ride for now, out of range then stop and think.*

They ride for an hour, well away from the small area where they all encountered the aroma. Looking around he says, "We need to talk."

Neither Stacey nor Holt question Ocher as they can see the stress in his face as he dismounts.

The group find a quiet place, off the trail. Firewood is gathered, the makings for coffee retrieved from the supply pack and a pot is on to boil.

Ocher walks just outside the camp. He stands alone, contemplating.

Before Ocher can say anything, Stacey says in a shaky voice, "It's them, isn't it?"

"I think so," Ocher answers. "There's no possible way they're here for... any of us."

"All the loose ends, as you call them, are here. Are you sure?" Holt asks.

"No. Not absolutely. The Tong is good, but not that good. If the remaining two assassins are here, they're after someone else. I can't leave and let them succeed. But.."

"Separating isn't a good choice. Is it?" Stacey continues.

"What are you all talking about?" Austin asks.

Ocher looks at Holt, then Stacey. Both nod their approval.

"Before coming to America, I was trained as an assassin. The people who trained me kidnapped Stacey, hoping to capture me. When we saved Stacey, the kidnappers told us that there were two assassins left. Those two are back there."

"What happened to the other men?" Austin asks.

"They died," Ocher states.

"Oh," Austin replies.

"My training took place on one of the islands in the Philippines. At age 16 I was assigned a contract to eliminate a man. I fulfilled that contract in Japan. It took three years. There I faked my death in a fire and escaped to this country. I changed my name and vowed not to use my skills as a professional ever again."

Austin turns toward Vernon, "Did you know about this?"

"A little bit," Vernon answers.

Ocher takes the cup of coffee in both hands and sips. "Something changed an hour ago. In the Philippines, rice is the main diet, rice with meat, fish or fowl. That's not unusual. It's the spices that go into the rice that makes the dish, and I know the smell of those spices all too well."

"Me too," Stacey adds. "I smelled those spices in that last encampment we went through. Ocher is right. I believe there's an assassin in that camp."

"We don't know who he or they are here for," Holt states, looking at the kids.

"He can't fulfill his contract if I can stop him. I also have to worry about all of you," Ocher finishes

Holt looks at Ocher, breaks a few small twigs and adds them to the fire. "I can't speak for Stacey, but I think she feels pretty much the same. The Governor of Texas once offered you a job as a Ranger, that makes you, at least in my mind, a Ranger. I don't abandon a fellow Ranger."

"We can't separate, so as I see it, we need to make some arrangements for these saddlebags, find a place to hold up and make a plan. Let's circle out east and go back to the Sheriff's cabin, or is that too far?" Stacey asks.

"You both know that I'll have to do this alone," Ocher says.

"Maybe," Stacey says. Then kicks dirt onto the fire.

"Well, I can at least hold the horses. Besides, I don't want to have to go back to Pine Creek and try and explain what the rest of you are doing," Holt adds as he dumps out the remaining coffee.

"An assassin," Austin says. "Really?"

"Not any more, Austin. Most everybody in the West was someone or something else at some other time. People change, mostly for the better. They want better for themselves and those around them. He's just in the process of that change. What say we stick around and make sure he don't go back to what he was," Holt says, looking at Austin and Vernon.

Ocher is speechless, can't look at Holt but is mighty glad and proud to have this man 'holding the horses' and to have Stacey at his side.

Chapter Eleven

They arrive back at the Sheriff's cabin at sunset and start making plans.

In the morning over the breakfast fire a plan is finalized, but not before a rather heated discussion is concluded. Will Ocher go alone?

"Won't it be better to have a man and his family camping out than a single man?" Stacey offers, after all have had their say.

"One mistake on my part and we could be facing the hostage situation again," Ocher counters.

"A man and his son would work. Wouldn't it, Uncle Ocher?" Vernon asks.

"I can act like a man," Austin argues.

"No, to the family. No, to you Austin. Vernon and I will go. No more discussion." Ocher sets his coffee cup down and stares down any further debate.

During the planning session, they all agree the probable target is Schuyler Colfax, the most senior envoy from Washington. *The question is:*

Where is the Colfax camp and how's he being guarded?

"I will ride in and meet with the Sheriff to discuss our concerns," Holt summarizes his role.

"Austin and I will stay here and guard the money," Stacey goes over their role.

"Vernon and I'll pick up the trail of the assassin," Ocher adds. "We'll meet back here in four days."

Ocher and Vernon set out on foot for the hike back to the area he suspects the assassin has temporarily made camp. The walk keeps them warm. Ocher knows that it's going to get cold, very cold.

They make their way by dozens of little camp communities. Fires, people making small talk, kids playing, the smell of cooking engulfs the air around the camps.

"Before we get too far, Vernon, you need to practice calling me Austin, not Uncle Ocher."

Vernon cocks his head to one side and smiles. "Those men might know your new name. Ok, Austin," Vernon responds.

They approach within a mile of the camp community of the assassin, then head due east, passing by more of the small temporary groups, finally heading up into the foothills to set up an observation post. Holt's advice not to work up a sweat, keeps the pace slow and steady. By mid-afternoon the pair are ensconced in camp.

The treaty signing has brought together hundreds of onlookers. From the vantage point Ocher can see dozens of little camps in the valley below. Each camp consists of three or four fire sites situated close to water and the main trail. He spends the day watching and noting every movement of each of the encampments that he and Vernon came close to. By sunset he knows the occupants of all the camps, including the exact location of the assassin. Vernon has organized the camp, gathered wood and has hot coffee ready.

The assassin's camp is well chosen, but with subtle differences; for access to the main road but also with an escape route. The assassin has placed four of his neighbors between the main road and his location. Anybody approaching will cause a disturbance, alerting him. There are no obstructions, human or terrain, blocking an obvious escape route. The camp sites adjacent to the assassin appear to be more permanent with supplies of fire wood and water in evidence.

The final clue is the fire. The assassin's fire is the only fire showing smoke. Old habits of a smoking fire to keep away mosquitoes are hard to break. Ocher also knows the occupant of the camp. For years he bullied Ocher into learning the assassin's craft.

He's known to Ocher as *Teacher*, the man who trained him. *Teacher is here, stalking.* Ocher spent ten years being trained to observe and strike. He's also spent ten years observing and learning about the Teacher. Ocher knows him and his weaknesses. When Ocher left the Philippine training camp, the Teacher had been the best, but only because Ocher was no longer there. Now Ocher would have to prove that to the Teacher.

The night is cold, even though the shelter is well built. Even with a fire, the cold is relentless. When the fire needs fuel, the shivering begins. In between stoking the fire and listening to Vernon's teeth chattering, Ocher has concluded two things. One: the Teacher has spent at least two days at the camp below. He will either leave tonight or first thing in the morning. Two: there's another camp, a fall back location with medical supplies, money and disguises to effect an escape.

Ocher will hunt the escape camp. He can always find the Teacher. In the morning his confidence about the assassin increases. The Teacher is gone. He's moving toward his target. The move is strategic.

"Vernon, let's pack up and get moving."

Vernon looks up from the fire and nods.

"Moving around will help get us warm." Ocher adds.

The cold slows Ocher's reflexes, stiffens the joints in his hands and overall makes him uncomfortable. Even standing in the sun doesn't help much.

"Where we going...Austin?" Vernon asks, holding his hands around the cup of hot coffee.

"Up there a ways," Ocher responds, pointing his chin toward the foothills, his hands around his own coffee cup. "I'll explain when we get moving."

They skirt the small camp communities finally in what seems, at least to Vernon, a silly move. They head higher. Higher and colder.

During a rest stop and sitting on a semi-warm rock Ocher explains, "That man back there has an escape camp. We're going to look for it."

Vernon sits quietly. Finally, he asks, "He would have to put it where other people wouldn't find it. Up here somewhere?"

"That's right."

"That means a cold camp. Doesn't it?" Vernon asks, a frown on his cold red forehead.

"Yep. A fire would stand out. Alerting him we're looking."

Vernon nods, pulling his coat collar higher.

They move higher into the mountain. They spend the day looking for a cave that is close to water with enough loose wood lying about that can be gathered without much effort and, most importantly, escape routes.

By mid-afternoon Ocher desperately wants to build a fire and have, if nothing else, some pine needle tea. Instead they stop for a bite of jerky and a cup of cold stream water.

Ocher knows he is close.

"Austin, look," Vernon points uphill from the rock they're sitting on.

One small upright pine bough with the white inner wood showing. Someone or something has moved the broken branch from the pine grove just down slope.

Ocher finishes his jerky but does not move to investigate. Instead he removes his spyglass and examines the area of the branch. One small mistake is all it takes; there is a small cave. The entrance has been covered over with pine boughs from the grove. All of the broken ends in the grove have been hidden with mud and all but one of the limbs has been pushed into the dirt.

"Good job, Vernon. I think you found his escape camp. What do you think we should do now?"

Vernon sits quietly, takes a drink of cold water, "Could have rigged some traps. But we still need to make sure."

"Good. That's exactly right. Let me go and check. You stay here for now. If I make a mistake, well... you know how to get back to the cabin, don't you?"

"I'll stay here 'till you signal me. I'd like to see the kind of traps," Vernon says.

Ocher suspects he knows the kind of traps the Teacher will use. There are small trip strings all around the cave. He gets just close enough to confirm his suspicions. The site meets all of the requirements he would set and with the aid of the spyglass he can see small bundles piled into the cave.

Ocher waves Vernon to the cave and spends several hours showing him the small but subtle trip traps.

"This man is good, Austin, but you are better," Vernon says, smiling at Uncle Ocher.

"What say we get down closer to civilization and set a camp, with a fire," Ocher asks.

"Yes sir."

They take the rest of the day moving out of the mountains and finding a camp site. At sunset they're sitting by a smokeless fire, each holding a hot cup of coffee more for warmth than the contents, although the coffee tastes mighty good. Before calling it a day, Ocher puts several heated rocks around their pine needle beds. Every little bit of heat helps.

Ocher and Vernon are moving well before dawn, too cold to stay put. During his surveillance and hunt for the escape camp he has had time to formulate how he would carry out an assassination. He has a day and a half before starting back to the Sheriff's cabin. By that time he will find the Teacher again.

Chapter Twelve

It takes only a day for Ocher to find the assassin again; it's the aroma of the spices that gives him away. Habits are the weakness that assassins look for and use against their prey. It seems Teacher would remember his own words.

They start back toward the cabin when it strikes Ocher, *this is too easy.* Holt's words come like a thunder clap. Watch your back trail. The cold has numbed not only his body but his mind.

The assassin English's last words flash through Ocher's mind. *There are only two of the Tong left. Is it possible that there are two assassins?*

Ocher and Vernon are well away from the Teacher so they stop. "I need to think on some things. You gather some wood and I'll get the coffee ready," Ocher requests.

Vernon needs no further encouragement, "Coffee sounds good."

After pouring both a cup of hot coffee, Ocher sits down near a log, his feet extended toward the fire. He reviews every detail of the last three days, but nothing indicates contact with a second assassin, although there was a complete day when Ocher was not observing the Teacher. Overconfidence is a killer. After finishing two cups of coffee and some jerky, Ocher leads them east away from civilization.

"We're going to make a big circle and come up to the cabin from the north, Vernon. If anyone is following us, we'll spot them."

Well after sunset they approach the Sheriff's cabin. A light is glowing through a window. It will be good to get warm and have a hot meal. They sit in the cold night for more than an hour observing.

Finally, Ocher hales the cabin. Holt responds and opens the door, "You two look like you could use something warm, amigo".

"You bet," is all Ocher can offer.

Vernon nods.

Austin is already offering Vernon a cup of coffee even before Stacey can do the same for Ocher.

The cabin is quiet while Vernon and Ocher warm up.

Stacey stands next to Ocher as he takes off his heavy coat.

"Glad you're back," she says, taking his coat and hanging it on the pegs next to the door. Vernon's coat is already hanging there.

"Sure could use a bowl of whatever that is cooking," Ocher says, pointing with his chin toward the stove.

Holt can wait no longer, "In a minute. Did you find him?"

"Yep, we found him," Ocher responds accepting a bowl of stew from Stacey. "Thanks. Things been ok here? Any trouble?"

"No trouble," Stacey responds. "Keeping Austin tied down takes a might of doing, but we managed."

"I got a bit of experience with that my own self," Ocher says, looking toward Vernon and Austin huddled together at the table.

"He's about to bust open," Stacey remarks glancing at Holt.

"Ok. What did you find out, Marshal?" Ocher asks through a grin.

"I met with the sheriff and told him we got word about the possibility of a murder attempt. Didn't tell him about you. We talked it over pretty good and came to the same conclusion; Schuyler Colfax is the only person out here that would warrant an attempt. One other thing, I know the Major in charge of the Army contingent accompanying Colfax. They're due here by the end of the week. We'll be able to talk with him then."

"You been busy. You both been busy. When is the treaty signing taking place?" Ocher asks.

"A week from Friday."

Ocher takes his bowl of stew, replenishes it and walks to the table. "If it was me, I would try before the signing. I don't believe the assassination has anything to do with the treaty. There'll be someone in the party that could sign in Colfax's place. So there's something else that warrants his death. We may never know who paid for the assignation, at least not from Teacher."

Austin looks up, "Who's the Teacher?"

Ocher tells them who Teacher is.

"How would you do it, Austin?" Vernon asks in between bites of stew.

"Austin?" Austin asks.

"We was afraid someone would recognize Uncle Ocher's real name so we used Austin instead," Vernon explains, proud to be part of the adventure.

"Yep, that's what we decided," Ocher confirms Vernon's assertion. "Now, here's what I'd do."

Holt shakes his head, "I would have never thought of that, but it makes perfect sense. How are you going to stop him? If he doesn't make the attempt, he's done nothing wrong."

"I don't know, but I have an idea. We'll need to talk to Colfax."

Ocher uses the next two days making sure that the cabin is safe. Using fishing and hunting as a guise, Ocher, Austin and Vernon take treks around the cabin taking the time to see who is camping close by. By the end of the week Ocher is confident that they're not being watched.

Friday morning over biscuits and bacon, Ocher asks, "Do we need any supplies?"

"No," Stacey responds. "There probably isn't much left anyway."

The night before Stacey, Austin and Vernon decided that they don't want to go into Fort Collins. "Too many people," Austin offers.

"I'd rather stay and fish," Vernon declares.

Friday, Ocher and Holt ride into town to meet with the sheriff and to see if the Colfax party has arrived at the fort. The closer they get the more dense the population gets. It's obvious, well before the two reach Fort Collins, that the dignitaries from Washington have arrived. Plus a huge part of the Sioux Nation.

The place is swarming like a bee hive. Ocher is reminded of St. Louis and the fact he didn't like it.

Ocher muses, *The sheriff will have his hands full before this is all over, even with the Army's help.*

The Deputy Sheriff is in the office when the pair arrive. "The Sheriff is over at the fort meeting with the Army big wigs."

Ocher and Holt try to ride over to see if they can get a word in with Major Kirby. They finally have to step down and lead the horses through the crowd. What should be a quick ride takes almost an hour.

Chapter Thirteen

Fort Collins is nothing but a fortified box full of people. You have to wait for someone to come out before you go in, or so it seems. Ocher and Holt manage to move through the mass and find where the meetings are taking place.

They wait outside until either the Sheriff or the Major walk by. Trying to get by the soldiers posted at the door seems too ambitious. Patience seems a more prudent approach. It works. After an hour Major Kirby and the Sheriff come out of the garrison door.

"Hello, Colonel," Major Kirby says to Holt.

"Good to see you, Bill. Have you got a minute?"

"Of course, Holt. Let's step back inside."

The Sheriff, Holt, Bill and Ocher step back into the building and into a small office.

"The Sheriff's already told me about your assassination plot, and as you know, I'm paid to take these things very seriously. Do you have more information for me before I talk to Mr. Colfax?"

Ocher introduces himself and gives Major Kirby the details he's learned over the past few days.

"Ocher, I won't ask how you know this man, but you seem pretty certain of your assessment, and if the Colonel thinks you're right, then you're right. What do we do?"

"Major, I have one more detail to take care of. Can we meet with you and Mr. Colfax tomorrow, same time, at your encampment?"

"That'll be fine. Colonel, I'll see you all tomorrow.   Sheriff, good luck. You'll need it," Kirby says as he dismisses the pair.

Chapter Fourteen

Ocher and Holt leave the overcrowded fort and head for the Sioux encampment. On the way Ocher explains to Holt, "I believe that our man will disguise himself as an Indian so he can move around freely without being challenged. If he can be identified, we can follow him and capture him in the act, hopefully."

The men enter the Sioux camp, find Red Bluff, and explain the situation to him.

"You wait here. The Elders will decide," Red Bluff says and leaves the camp fire.

It doesn't take long until Red Bluff returns. "They agree. Scouts will leave now. They will find this man and you will be told. We will watch him."

"I know your scouts are brave and fearless, Red Bluff, but this man has spent his whole life learning to kill. Do not engage him in battle. He will win."

"How you know this?" Red Bluff asks.

"He trained me," Ocher responds.

Red Bluff just grunts an understanding, finally, "Geronimo pick good blood brother. Only my most skilled trackers will be sent out."

"Thank you, Red Bluff."

The mass of people camping around Fort Collins is overwhelming and it appears to be getting more crowded by the moment. Moving through the crowd takes the remainder of the day.

The pair arrive back at the Sheriff's cabin at sunset. There are people camping around the cabin but at least no one had taken up residence inside the small horse shelter. Both men are astounded by the number of people drawn to the treaty signing. The evening goes quietly by without incident, even with all the small camps set up around the cabin.

The security of the cabin and the saddlebags is becoming a concern.

Chapter Fifteen

At dawn, Ocher starts out of the cabin to fetch water for coffee and finds two Sioux Braves sitting on the front stoop. "Red Bluff say to come."

A quick breakfast is prepared and eaten. Ocher and Holt leave for Red Bluff's Camp. Ocher convinces the two braves to stay and guard the cabin. The braves agree to watch the cabin from outside as neither had ever spent the night inside a building.

Ocher and Holt work their way through the ever-swelling mass of people and arrive to meet with Red Bluff around noon.

Over antelope stew, Red Bluff explains, "He is here as you thought. My best warriors are watching, but not seen. If this coward is to attack the important man, the best time would be in two nights. No moon."

The Sioux Warrior is a shrewd tactician knowing the virtue of darkness. Ocher will never under-estimate the Chief, but is even more impressed with his understanding of the "hunt" every time they meet.

"I'll meet with Mr. Colfax today and explain to him that he's being hunted. We have to capture this man in the act of his attempt, or he'll go free." Red Bluff doesn't understand the concept of 'The Law' but does understand the hunt.

Schuyler Colfax is not a big man nor a man accustomed to the outdoors, especially the West. He's a man of offices, court rooms, and he's out of place in this environment.

"Gentlemen, come in. Please be seated," Mr. Colfax says, in a cordial, polite and surprisingly calm voice.

Even more surprising is his calm demeaner after hearing about the plan for his assassination.

"I may be out of my element right now, but in business and politics I am as tough as any man. Over the years, I have ruined many a man and their reputation. Some deserved it and some perhaps didn't. The fact that someone would pay to have me killed is no surprise. I won't change my ways to avoid the attempt. I'm here on behalf of President Andrew Jackson, and I intend to accomplish the task he's entrusted to me. I'll leave this assassin to you men as you are more suited to that endeavor. If that's all, I have a great deal to do before the signing. Good day to you. Thank you for coming and bringing this to my attention."

It was over: no discussion, no change of schedules, no extra care. The man is tougher than he appears. Not a man to cross, at least in his world. The rest is being left to Ocher, Holt, Major Kirby, Sheriff Walsenburg and the Sioux Nation.

Ocher speaks up, "Gentlemen, we know where the hunter and the hunted are. The rest should be easy." All the men realize the irony of the statement as they plan for the capture of Teacher.

Chapter Sixteen

The night is frigid, moonless and windless. Ocher's plan is in place. The only real unknown is the possible existence of a second killer. If he were to use a second man, it would be to create a diversion and that contingency has also been accounted for. Now only patience is needed.

Ocher can hear the dog bark given off by one of the Sioux braves watching the assassin, alerting the group that Teacher is moving toward Schuyler Colfax's tent.

Ocher moves to the tent, slices an entrée slit in a side wall and slips into the sleeping area of the partitioned tent. He waits.

The sound is barely audible, a very sharp knife slicing through the opposite side wall of the tent. Ocher waits then speaks from behind the high backed rocking chair. "Good evening, Teacher."

The only sound is that of a knife striking the head rest of the rocking chair.

Schuyler Colfax sits upright on his cot, strikes a match, lights an oil lamp and looks directly at Ocher, then at the knife sticking in his rocking chair's headrest and the black clad man standing across from Ocher.

The Teacher smiles and shifts his eyes just slightly, looking past Ocher, then dives toward the slit Ocher made in the tent when he entered. Immediately Ocher realizes the implication of the move, the lamp. "Hit the ground," he shouts at Colfax just as an explosion shatters the night. Glass shrapnel rips through the tent. As the Teacher races past, Ocher manages to slice through the escaping man's thigh with the knife he carries between his shoulder blades.

Colfax stands and grabs the blanket from the cot and puts out the fire from the broken oil lamp. Major Kirby rushes in holding a torch in a blood soaked right hand. Ocher's only comment is "He's wounded but has escaped. How many are injured?"

"Are you all right, Mr. Colfax?" the Major asked excitedly.

"Yes, I'm fine. How many are injured?"

"Nobody, thanks to Ocher's advice about a diversion. Should we go after him?"

Ocher places the razor sharp knife back in the sheath between his shoulder blades. "I'll go. Alone."

"Sergeant, let's get some more light in here," Kirby turns and shouts out.

Colfax looks at Major Kirby's bloody hand, "Sergeant, get the Doctor as well."

"Yes, sir," is the only response.

Colfax breaks the silence, "Major, if you would be so kind, have someone repair the tent. Gentlemen, thank you all for your concern and actions of this evening. I need my rest."

Chapter Seventeen

"**M**r. Colfax, you're still in danger. But I'm pretty sure we can determine as to why and who wants you dead. Right here and right now," Ocher states.

Colfax takes a long hard look at Ocher. "You couldn't possibly know that."

"You are correct, sir, but the Major does."

Major Kirby reacts immediately. "You can't be serious. What have I to gain? I'm incensed that you could even think that. The Colonel has known me for years. This is insane."

Holt moves next to Major Kirby and removes his sidearm. "Ocher, what proof do you have for this accusation?"

Schuyler Colfax starts to sit down in his rocking chair but can't due to the knife in the head rest. His stare is focused on Ocher. "Young man, you better be right. You are about to ruin an officer's career."

Ocher stares directly in Major Kirby's face. "At our first meeting, you used the term assassins. Hoyt used the term murder plot. I thought it was a grammatical error, but it wasn't. You were speaking about more than one assassin. The fact that you met them face to face is going to cost you your life."

Holt moves to the other side of Kirby just in case he tries to draw his sword.

"You never questioned the fact that I thought the assassins would disguise himself as an Indian. You had seen that their complexion would match that of an Indian. So you already knew they would blend in."

From the front of the tent two men enter the sleeping area, the sergeant and a tall, thin, sallow complexioned man carry a medical bag.

"Doctor, please check the Major's wound," Colfax orders.

The Doctor takes a cursory look at the bleeding hand, "You called me here for that?"

Ocher seeing the impatience of the man, "Take a close look, sir. Note the blue discoloration of the hand. The Major will not see the sunrise."

The doctor puts down his bag and reexamines the hand. "Looks like a simple bruise to me. What makes you say this wound is fatal?"

"Kirby, how did you get the cut on your hand?" Ocher asks.

"Just a small splinter."

"Be patient, Doctor. I'll get to that in a moment." Ocher states. "Let me continue. I thought it was odd that you allowed Mr. Colfax to camp out among the crowd, even with guards. You somehow played to his ego that he should be out here with the people and easier to get at."

"My ego," Colfax considers the comment for a moment. "You would be correct, Ocher. My ego overtook my common sense."

"The last two bits of the puzzle came together in here. When Teacher came into the tent, he made no attempt at Colfax. He came after me. He knew I was here, because you told him about me, Kirby."

The Major's demeanor shows that he's accepted the fact he has been caught. His shoulders and head are down, his breathing has increased and he's sweating in the cold air.

"Finally, it's your hand. It won't stop bleeding, will it?"

Kirby just shakes his head.

"Once you met face to face with the assassins they could not afford to let you live. I suspect that one of the men was short, maybe five foot tall."

Kirby again acknowledged the fact with a nod of the head.

"His nickname is Scorpion. He is a master with poisons. The splinter you removed from your hand was soaked with octopus venom. You are going to bleed to death Kirby, from the inside. Your blood will not clot. There is no cure or antidote for the poison."

Colfax sees that the Major has conceded to the accusation. "Why, Kirby?"

"My father's name was Stevens. Kirby is my mother's, from North Carolina."

Colfax just shakes his head. "Brian Stevens. I had him tried for treason and hanged. Was that your father?"

"It was, so I took my mother's name and joined the Union Army as a spy and to get close to you."

"I have no regrets about your father. He was a traitor. If Ocher is correct, and I am sure he is, I will not get the privilege of having you hanged," Colfax was now taking charge of the moment.

"Doctor, I leave the Major in your care. Kirby, please surrender your sword to the Colonel."

Holt, sensing what's about to happen, says, "Mr. Colfax, I'm no longer a Colonel."

"That is true. But you were, and as I understand it, a very good one." Colfax continues, "My security detail requires an officer. Thanks to you and that gentlemen," pointing toward Ocher, "there is now a vacancy in that position."

"Promote the Sergeant," Holt counters.

"I have tried on more than one occasion to promote the Sergeant into the officer's ranks, and he has declined. I need a proven leader to take charge of the military detail accompanying me. I am requesting your services."

"Do I have a choice, sir?"

"Not really. The Governor of Texas is a friend. I'm sure that won't be a problem."

Holt tries to speak, "But..."

Colfax cuts him off. "Sergeant, do you think you can gather the appropriate accoutrements to outfit a Colonel?"

It takes all of the Sergeant's effort to speak through the grin on his face. "It will be my pleasure. Welcome back, Colonel."

Colfax is in his element now, "It's too late to go back to sleep. Sergeant, please wake my staff at the fort and have them come here. I have telegrams to send and a speech to finish. Ocher, would you please give me a moment?"

Ocher follows Colfax through the meeting space of the tent and into the sleeping area. "Mr. Jones, Ocher, thank you for stopping this assassination attempt. I won't ask about your obvious association with that man, just to say I'm glad you're on our side now. I would ask for one indulgence. I'd like to retain possession of the knife. It's going to make a great story in Washington. If you ever need my kind of assistance, do not hesitate to ask." With that Ocher is dismissed.

"Mr. Colfax, you're not safe yet. The assassin who came in here, Teacher, is wounded. How bad I don't know. I will follow him. Scorpion will probably come for you now. I will brief Holt, the Colonel, how to keep you out of harm's way until I return to deal with him."

"One day, Ocher, I would be interested to hear your story."

"Perhaps one day, sir." Ocher turns and leaves.

Chapter Eighteen

Ocher steps out from the relative warmth of the tent into the intense cold. "Well, Colonel, let's talk about Scorpion."

"Don't call me Colonel. What about him?"

"Teacher is hurt and will head to his get-a-way camp. Red Bluff's braves are camped there so he can't get to his supplies. That gives me the advantage. I'll find him. Scorpion knows I'll pursue Teacher, so he'll attempt to complete the assassination. You have to keep Colfax at a distance from... well, everybody. To complete the kill he'll have to get close enough to introduce some type of poison. Remember he is only five feet tall and very quick. Keep Colfax surrounded with people you know."

"That will be next to impossible," Holt replies. "I thought I knew Kirby. I'll conscript some of the fort's people. I'll put the money in the safe at the fort and the supply clerk will hold it until you return. Ocher, good luck."

"Good luck to us both, Colonel."

Ocher moves into the cold night toward the fires of Red Bluff's encampment. Even the taciturn Chief will be curious about the explosion and the events of the evening. Ocher knows how he wants to deal with Teacher. What he doesn't know is the terrain, but Red Bluff does.

The camp would normally be docile, but not this evening. There's a buzz of anticipation as Ocher enters the camp. The braves are too polite to ask about what has happened. They wait patiently as Ocher tells the story and then reveals his plan for Teacher.

Red Bluff listens patiently as Ocher explains his pursuit. The Chief has seen many battles and is a brilliant tactician. He points out several flaws in the plan, but agrees with the premise. Keep Teacher moving and exposed to the elements. The cold and snow are weapons that Teacher has never faced and Ocher will use them to his advantage.

Red Bluff and Ocher spend several hours finalizing the operation. The dirt around the camp fire is filled with drawings of the terrain. Ocher is even more impressed with Red Bluff's understanding of battle tactics when the meeting is concluded. He's thankful he is not trying to chase the old Indian through the mountains.

The plan is simple - keep Teacher moving in the elements, herding him toward a choke point where Ocher will confront the assassin. Red

Bluff's braves will surround the prey and provide only one way to go.

Ocher's in no hurry as he puts together his meager supplies. The longer he stays warm and Teacher has to deal with the elements, the better. After a hardy breakfast of oatmeal and biscuits with ham, he starts moving northwest. He will spend the rest of the day getting ahead of the escaping assassin. Teacher can't conceive that Ocher or the Indians have the skill to outflank him. Red Bluff's braves will allow themselves to be seen just enough to stoke Teacher's arrogance. Ocher knows from experience that, if the braves do not wish to be seen, they won't be.

Ocher has the patience to wait in ambush where Teacher will try to escape, recover and return to the assignment. Ocher intends to impede all of those efforts.

Chapter Nineteen

Ocher, now dressed in his buckskin shirt, pants, and jacket, along with fur lined moccasins, steps into the saddle. The confrontation with the assassins is days away maybe longer, but he is ready. Ocher knows that Red Bluff's braves could hunt down these men and kill them but as Ocher explained, "This is not your fight."

Red Bluff's only comment is to sweep his hand across the horizon and say, "Our people will have their fill of death. This paper we will sign. It will not stop the dying."

Ocher is ready. His only regret is that he has lied to Holt. The hunt is not for one man but two. Colfax's assassination can wait. Ocher has now become the number one target, because you don't just quit the Tong, at least not alive. He thinks to himself, *Those two arrogant flatlanders think they have the advantage.* He laughs out loud. *I'm even beginning to talk like a Westerner.*

The two braves who are with Ocher turn and look at him and just shake their heads. *Crazy white man.*

The three men move west by south all day. By sunset they have also climbed into the mountains and into the cold. Tomorrow Ocher will begin the hunt on his own.

The cold is an enemy he is not accustomed to. It does not attack with subtlety, just brute force with no escape. Cold was described to him, but reality is much different.

The night camp is compact with a small fire built in a hollow surrounded by downed trees. An intruder would discover it only by stumbling into it. Ocher watches the braves to learn the little things to keep him alive and is glad he's not pursuing these men. The temperature seems to be an inconvenience to them whereas it's an intense mental battle for Ocher.

The warmth of the fire is barely keeping the freezing cold from invading the camp. These two are testing him. He's determined to meet their challenge because he knows that the challenge ahead of him will be far worse than this.

The morning is dismal with low hanging misty clouds full of freezing, wet cold. Visibility is almost nothing. You can imagine bears, mountain lions or assassins just out of view. His coffee is good. The braves decline the offer and the warmth of the fire is very good.

The older of the two braves points, "Keep white trees to your right shoulder until no more trees. Snow come today and tonight. Keep fire small, sleep close. Watch pony. He smarter than you." They both move out of camp and are immediately enveloped by the mist. Ocher looks over at the pony. He's decided to take the Indian pony and leave the Pinto just in case he makes a fatal mistake. "That was short and to the point."

Ocher's strategy session with Red Bluff was to get ahead of the two assassins at a natural choke point. The braves will try and move the two men to Ocher. If for some reason they escape the push, Red Bluff will send a brave to tell him of the failure. Ocher had asked, "How will they find me?" Red Bluff just laughs.

The day proceeds. Move for half a mile or so, stop, listen for minutes, always expecting something to appear in the mist, then move again, the cold always finding a way to creep in. At noon, or what Ocher considers noon, he stops, makes a small fire and debates over making coffee. He finally decides the coffee will warm him some and he can pee on the fire when he leaves and not have to relieve himself in the cold.

There are towering mountains to his west. He knows that, as soon as the sun goes below the mountain top, the temperature will start to drop. It will get dark quickly, so the hunt for a secure camp site begins not long after his noon stop. His breath has frozen on his face and eyebrows.

Moving is an effort. All of his joints seem not to function. Simple tasks like gathering fuel and starting a fire have to be well thought out. He finally finds what he's looking for: a camp on the west side of a small valley where the sun will hit early. The site looks east and is above the valley giving him a vantage point. There's a natural corral behind his overhang where he can let the pony run free.

Just as he starts to bring in fire wood the snow starts. He gathers much more than he thinks he'll need and then gathers more because Red Bluff said it's never enough. He pays no attention to his tracks, by the time he gets the fire going all remnants of his presence are under the snow. He does make one final trek out of his camp cutting a wide semi-circle to see if the fire is visible, sets a couple of rabbit snares and checks on the pony. Finally satisfied that he's as safe as he can get, Ocher settles in over coffee, cold biscuits and hot bacon.

During the night the snow and mist lift and the day is bright and sunny. He has already decided to continue his hunt on foot. Stalking on horseback is not a comfortable thought. He will use this place as a base camp, leaving the pony. There's water and feed in the corral area. If he doesn't make it back, the pony can escape easily enough. Below his lair is a river. Ocher takes the time to haul up river rocks and replaces the stones in his fire pit, just in case he gets outflanked. When heated, the stones will explode.

Ocher takes only a blanket, coffee cup, jerked beef, knife and his Sharpes and moves to the edge of the overhang. He sits just inside the shelter acclimating to the cold and methodically scans the valley with his telescope. Over an hour later he steps out on the ledge, works into the tree line and starts moving east, knowing his prey are doing the same. The only difference is they're not prepared for the common enemy, the cold.

Ocher stays on the west side of the valley where the sun is melting the snow. He stays behind a ridgeline and periodically moves to the top and surveys the valley. He's not traveling with speed in mind. He has decided that the two assassins know he's in pursuit and they will try to bracket him. In addition, he will give them the high ground, the higher the better. The higher they go, the colder it gets.

He does stop for a cup of pine tea with a bit of beef slivers thrown in around noon but keeps moving, always watching and anticipating a mistake. Hoping the mistake will not be his. The ever present companion close at hand, the cold.

Well before sunset he has made camp in a clump of deadfalls that he has covered with pine boughs. The branches will keep the heat in and dissipate any smoke from a fire. He does not break off any of the dead branches of the dead falls. The snapping of the wood can be heard a great distances. During the night the cold invites a friend, the wind.

The wind forces the cold onto any and every unprotected patch of skin. There is no protection from the invasion. The day proceeds exceedingly slow. Move for a few minutes, find the leeward side of anything, observe the surrounds, catch your breath and move on. As much discomfort as Ocher is experiencing, he knows the other two are enduring at a greater cost.

Just before his noon camp the first mistake occurs, a brief one but still a mistake, smoke. Someone has started a fire and the wind has gotten to it, stoking it into a blaze. Realizing the error they have thrown snow on the fire to extinguish it and a plume of white smoke has resulted.

Not a mistake a Westerner or an Indian would make.

Ocher stops, moves into a small protected hollow and watches. He's not exposed to the wind but the cold sets in. He won't make a fire and definitely won't give up this advantage, so he sits and suffers. During the remainder of the day, Ocher has identified a likely spot to cross the ridge. He has calculated the exact route to the crossing site, memorizing each step. At full dark he will make the move. Once behind the hill he will make a small fire and drink as much pine tea as possible then relocate for the night. It will be a risk to move but a bigger risk if his small fire is spotted.

He has also observed both men as they have leap frogged through the valley. They are currently separated by approximately two miles being as cautious with their movement as their capabilities will allow. Ocher has seen that they are not prepared for this climate. They are actually overdressed for their movements. Moving quickly they are sweating in their clothing and the sweat is freezing against their skin when they stop, evidenced by the fires they start every time one of them stops and signals to the other. *Patience is now the key. Let the elements work.*

After getting warm or as warm as he can get next to the small fire, Ocher takes a shallow angle going from tree to tree and painstakingly moves down the ridge. The clouds seem to wait for him to clear the temporary camp before allowing the moon to seep into the valley. He immediately takes the exact opposite angle and again moves from tree to tree, the moonlight lighting the way. Finally he finds a small cave on the down slope and steps in. He begins to heat several pancake sized flat mountain rocks while having broth.

During the night he sleeps on two of the stones while the other two heat in the coals exchanging them when the chill wakes him. At daybreak he has had a reasonably warm and comfortable night. Ocher is in place atop the ridge next to a large rock with the sun coming up behind him, telescope in place and sheltered from the wind.

Chapter Twenty

The two men have made separate camps but now are moving toward each other. *Why?* He doubts that he has been spotted. Suddenly between the two men a small herd of deer break cover and race downhill. Each assassin ducks for cover, still miles from each other. Ocher scans the area where the deer broke cover but can see nothing. *There, a small fire, someone is between the two men, but who. Not an Indian. They would never flush out deer and then build a visible fire.* Ocher scours the side of the mountain meticulously inch by inch but can see no one. The fire has died out and the two assassins have gone to ground still separated.

Ocher stays almost motionless pondering the events, concluding that the assassins thought they had bracketed him and were moving in for the kill when the unknown person flushed the deer in order to stop the two men. The only logical answer is Holt. He's the only person who knows about the situation. Ocher thinks to himself, *You should have stayed safe and warm with Colfax.*

Opportunity comes in many forms, confusion being one of them. Across the valley there are at least two men attempting to determine if they are still the aggressors. Ocher decides to add to the confusion. A misty fog has rolled into the valley and he takes full advantage and crosses the still flowing river inadvertently getting one foot wet.

He bellies under a grove of spruce trees and listens for any sound natural or unnatural. Satisfied that his movements have gone unnoticed, he starts crawling across the pine straw but stops and moves back. Why he doesn't grasp right away but something stops him. A single grain of rice but why here. Trip wires, Teacher's favorite. While setting the trap, Teacher must have set down his kit, spilling the contents. That's what Ocher has done around his own camp just as he has been taught.

Ocher sits in the natural den of the spruce grove debating on how to proceed, drying his wet foot with pine needles. Ocher dismantles the trip wire, observing that the trap is a warning devise not a weapon. One of the two assassins must have a camp close by and has set up warning devices around the perimeter. Within minutes Ocher finds the camp and several other noise makers. This camp would make Ojos laugh; this man is no frontiersman, leaving sign everywhere.

The camp is sheltered from the weather but poorly organized. The fire is large, somewhat concealed with a big fire pit but no extra fuel. There are no bones or other scrapes of food in the charcoal. There's been no attempt to insulate his sleeping area from the cold ground. This man is lying directly on the ground losing all body heat. A haversack with some supplies is casually hidden next to a tree. *It is Teacher's. He'll return, if for no other reason than to pick up the pack. The cold is having the intended effect. Teacher is making poor judgments and decisions, but he's still dangerous, very dangerous.*

Ocher must find Holt. But first, a little surprise. Ocher goes back to the river and returns with three river rocks that are almost an exact match of three rocks in the fire pit. After switching the stones he retraces his steps and returns to his vantage point on the opposite side of the valley.

Ocher returns to his rock and settles down to observe the camp across the valley. The mist turns to rain then to snow, back to rain but remains a constant: miserable. He's finally rewarded by the flicker of a fire in the assassin's camp. He waits. The explosion isn't loud but loud enough to know that the river rocks have heated up the absorbed water, expanding the stones to create flying fragments. Certainly not a trick taught in the jungle.

Ocher has already decided that he will take the offensive regardless of the camp fire explosion. Teacher will be on the alert and maybe hurt worse, but Ocher is tired of the cold and the deadly game. Up to now the two assassins have worked apart but the noise of the explosion could bring Scorpion closer in. All the better.

Ocher waits until an incoming tide of cold mist rolls through the valley then he crosses the stream. Taking each step with caution he works through the islands of White Birch and Fir trees. He knows that each step is closing the distance to death, a reality that would come sooner or later. His future is about living and all the pleasures life offers. The assassins, their future will end today.

The Teacher will use a diversion before any attack. He always does. He disguises the fact that he is left handed, fighting an opponent with a right handed stance until the last moment then switches to the dominant left side for the ending attack.

Ocher stops to observe the terrain. The most convenient attack location will be level ground coming from ambush or out of a concealed blind. Too face to face for the Teacher. From behind or above will be his choice. Ocher cuts an Aspen pole of approximately eight feet long and sharpens one end. Using the pole as a walking staff, he keeps the pointed end up, knowing that if the Teacher tries to come from above out of the trees or a rock ledge he will not enjoy the greeting he will receive. Now it's up to Ocher's years of training, moving slowly forward five to ten paces at a time, looking for a trip wire or dead fall. Each pause he turns to watch his back trail.

When a wave of mist comes down the valley Ocher changes position, never maintaining a straight course. If the Teacher is watching, each time the mist rolls through, Ocher disappears.

It is always the small things that change the course of history or destiny. Teacher's destiny changes as a result of dripping water, too much dripping. Just ahead of Ocher's intended route is an outcropping of rock. He was going to step through and continue up the valley but the water dripping from the other side of the outcrop is inconsistent with the surroundings. Teacher is on top and on the other side. His clothes have absorbed the mist and are shedding the water. Ocher stops under the outcrop as a bank of mist creeps in.

Where is Scorpion? Let Teacher wait. Concentrate on Scorpion. After the mist subsides Ocher slowly scans the surrounding area until he is satisfied that only Teacher is close by, less than ten feet directly above. Ocher steps out in the open, hesitates but only for an instant, then takes five quick steps and turns, bringing the staff parallel to the ground.

Teacher, expecting to deliver a devastating attack from his perch, is taken by surprise and is off balance when he hits the ground. Ocher lunges with the sharpened Aspen pole, aiming directly at Teacher's throat. Teacher deflects the thrust with a downward knife hand defense breaking the spear but not before the tip inflicts a laceration from neck to belly, bloody but not fatal.

"Finally, Little Orphan, we will test your resolve." The Teacher uses Ocher's Tong name.

Ocher drops the broken spear and moves slightly to his left, keeping his leading foot outside of Teacher's leading foot, avoiding a direct assault and forcing Teacher from a right hand stance to a left hand stance. Ocher anticipates the change and attacks over the extended right arm: a closed fist to the right side of Teacher's jaw. He twists his fist at impact, opening up a gash.

Teacher, trying to adopt a better defensive position, changes his stance again. Ocher waits for the move and attacks straight in to the jaw with the heel of his hand. The assassin staggers backward and falls into a sitting position. Ocher does not move in, knowing that the fall is intentional. Teacher stands, and, with the natural move of standing, hurls a throwing knife at Ocher.

In any confrontation, to walk away untouched is not plausible. Ocher accepts that as part of the conflict. Deciding how much damage and where it can least affect you is a critical calculation. Ocher cannot escape the knife. His left hand is not critical to the engagement so he takes the knife through the left hand. In as quick a motion as Teacher's, Ocher withdraws the knife and throws it back at his assailant, striking him in the left shoulder just above the collar bone. "If it's poison, we both die."

Both men stand gauging the other, blood dripping from them both, staining the snow while the mist flows around them. Each move is countered by the other. Ocher has studied Teacher for years, *Impatience is his flaw.*

Ocher makes the conscious choice to provide an opening for Teacher to attack, knowing that Teacher will see the move as a miscalculation. Ocher has kept on the outside of Teacher's lead foot but now steps directly in front. Teacher reacts by turning to deliver a round house fist. As he pivots around, he loses sight of Ocher for a millisecond, allowing Ocher to step forward blocking the blow with his chest. More importantly it allows Ocher an opening to deliver a closed fist punch to Teacher's jaw as he comes around to refocus on Ocher. The momentum of the turn is doubled by Ocher's full weight behind the punch.

Ocher's punch lands ahead of the round house fist. The impact on Ocher is far more devastating than he expects. It drives the wind out of him and knocks him backward. He fights to remain conscious but can't. His last thought before the black consumes him is: *I hope Scorpion doesn't find me.* He's not worried about Teacher following up an attack because he knows that Teacher's neck broke on impact.

Upon regaining consciousness he notes that the weather has not changed. The mist has settled and frozen on his clothing. To stand is an all-out effort. Every joint and muscle protest: the cold has literally frozen all of his moving parts. What starts as an attempt at standing becomes a slow and painful trek. He slides laterally to a rock to stabilize before continuing the agonizing journey. The ice and snow provide a slick surface, helping him slide along the ground. What seems like hours later he's behind the hill and still struggling to stand.

He has never experienced this level of helplessness or pain. The simple act of standing and taking a step tasks every bit of his physical and mental strength. Leaning against a tree he sets a goal of getting to the next tree then the next. He realizes he cannot stay in the open and sets the ultimate goal: return to his base camp.

After hours of suffering, he now can walk with only the occasional aid of a tree of bush. He can't hold a thought. His mind wanders. The cold doesn't seem to be as severe. A nap seems appropriate but instinct tells him not to stop and sleep. He's amazed as he nears the base camp to see the pony watch him approach. *Odd,* he thinks, *the pony isn't looking at me but in a different direction.* Adrenalin rushes through Ocher's system as he realizes that the pony is watching someone else. He drops to the ground just a small bamboo arrow passes through the space Ocher has just occupied.

He can hold a thought now, *The Scorpion has arrived.* Ocher must attack before the cold overcomes him again. Staying low, he moves toward the scrub bush and the trees on an upslope trying to gain the high ground and loosen up his muscles. Just as he gains the tree line he hears a grunt of alarm and turns to see the small assassin tangled in one of the rabbit snares. Turning quickly, Ocher charges directly at the Scorpion wanting to end the confrontation. The assassin disregards his tangled foot, raises his crossbow and aims directly at the oncoming Ocher.

Out of the low scrub brush to the left of the Scorpion, a figure rises and, with a practiced stroke, slashes the assassin across the throat with a small sword but not before the crossbow is discharged. Ocher first thought, *Where did Holt get a waist sword.* He rushes forward just in time to see the figure turn and face him. Two facts strike him. One: it isn't Holt. Two: the bamboo arrow of the crossbow in lodged in the man's neck.

Abel Jones smiles as he casually grasps the arrow and removes it from his neck. "Hope you brought some tea. I really do hate coffee." Both

men, ignoring the obvious, know what the
outcome of the poisoned arrow will be.

"As a matter of fact I did and some honey as
well," Ocher responds, trying not to let his voice
break.

The men step over the body of the Scorpion
and move into the shelter of the cave. Ocher
starts a fire, melting snow in the coffee pot to
make tea. "I better go move the debris outside
before we draw in something hungry. Here's the
tea and a cup. You'll have to heat the honey a
bit."

Ocher drags the assassin's body several
hundred yards away from the camp dropping it
into a crevice in the rock and pushing snow,
scree and logs on top. He feels no remorse about
the death of the little man. His only thought is
about Abel.

"The weather is worsening. I'd best gather
some more wood," Ocher says, as he piles fuel in
the corner before he steps back out of the cave.
By the time he makes half a dozen fire wood
trips and thanks the pony for being more alert
than he was, the snow is blowing horizontally
down the valley.

Ocher has volumes of questions to ask and
knows that time is evaporating quickly so he
finally asks, "The waist sword you used. It has
an emblem on it. Is it yours?"

Abel Jones looks up from his tea and smiles.
"Good a place to start as any. Yes, it's mine along

with my tattoo, same as yours. I will say that Ocher suits you better than Little Orphan."

"I suspected as much from the beginning," Ocher points toward Abel's cup. "The tea. No self-respecting mountain man drinks tea."

"Never got the taste for coffee, so I never changed. Besides never stayed close to civilization for folks to notice."

"How do know about Little Orphan?"

"I gave you the name. Found you and your parents in our jungle. Your folks died of some kind of fever so I brought you to the Tong. Stayed long enough to make sure they wouldn't just kill you. I wanted out, so I left."

"It wasn't by chance that we met out in the desert, was it?"

"Nope. George Stanley wrote me that you were in America. Your folks seemed to be the peaceful sort. I found notebooks with drawings of birds, lizards plants and such. With their blood in you it seemed probable that you'd be peaceful as well. Even with your training I figured you would get out first chance that come up. So I told Mr. Stanley to keep an eye out for you. Him and several other folks up and down the coast. You just happened to come to the same port as I did."

"You've been following me ever since," Ocher stated.

"Yep. One thing if you don't' mind."

"Of course," Ocher replies.

"A while back I mentioned I was headed to the Sands of Many Colors. Remember?"

"Yes."

"Just south of Blue Sands, where we met, there's a big valley. There's wood made of stone. I call it the Sands of Many Colors. Can you take me there?"

"Yes," Ocher says, but Abel Jones never hears the answer.

Chapter Twenty-One

The cave that previously seemed large enough to accommodate both men now seems to close in around Ocher. His emotions can find no solid ground. Anger, sadness, defeat, and success rush at him. The answer comes to him from the serene figure of his friend and the pledge he has made to Abel.

The night evaporates into dawn. Setting his emotions aside, Ocher wraps Abel in a blanket.

Ocher doesn't try to find Abel's camp. He could find it but the hunt will take too much time. He prepares for the trek back to Fort Collins. There's no sleep for Ocher. The caldron of emotions continues to boil. The loss of Abel, the loss of parents he never actually knew but now misses, the prospect of his own family. Sleep is impossible so he sits and plans for the trip to the Sands of Many Colors.

At first light Ocher cuts several long Aspen poles and fashions a travois. There's no need for a fire as Ocher has no interest in eating. He just wants to get his friend out of the mountains. By noon and under a clear sky Ocher leads the pony toward the trail leading back to Fort Collins.

He has no concept of time. The pony takes the lead, Ocher following in between the parallel marks of the travois. They stop occasionally to rest, build a fire for coffee and Ocher even drinking some of it but not much. He isn't sure when they come into the camp where the braves are waiting. All of a sudden he's there.

When Ocher's emotions clear, he's sitting at a camp fire with Red Bluff at his side. In the periphery Ocher can hear movement and talking. The Chief hands him a clay bowl, "Eat, so you may continue your journey." Ocher absently lifts the bowl to his mouth, realizing it is some kind of stew. He also realizes he's hungry. "Where is Abel Jones?" he asks.

"My braves have taken his body to Fort Collins to have it prepared. His spirit is with you."

"Thank you."

"The man you call Jones is known as a friend and honored enemy to all of the Nations. It is our obligation to honor him as it is your obligation to take his body to his sacred place. Rest today and begin tomorrow."

Red Bluff stands and leaves Ocher sitting by the fire still unsettled with his emotions.

Without Ocher knowing, another someone has taken the place of Red Bluff. "Ocher, we are ready to go, when you are," Stacey says.

Ocher is jerked from his reverie. "How... when did you get here?"

"Red Bluff sent for us. We are all here, Ocher."

For the first time in his life Ocher realizes that he needs someone and he is not alone.

Red Bluff returns to sit with Ocher and Stacey. "All of the Nations know of Abel Jones. At a time of mourning and celebration, all of the Human Beings tolerate each other. If you wish, I will go with you to Jones' sacred place."

"I will think on that, Red Bluff," Ocher replies, reaching for Stacey's hand.

Red Bluff grunts his understanding.

Chapter Twenty-Two

Fort Collins has returned to its normal raucous self now that the dignitaries have gone. The snow of the mountains is rain down on the plateau, turning the streets into wallows. Wagon wheel tracks don't last but a second before filling in.

The demeanor of the riffraff has changed as well. During the signing there were no muttered insults about the Indians but now the tolerance has evaporated.

When Ocher arrives at the Sheriff's office, there are two drifters standing on the porch. One of the men makes an offhanded comment about Red Bluff. Ocher stiffens and starts to reply.

"There are important things to attend to. Let it pass," Stacey says, placing her hand on Ocher's arm.

Ocher steps back immediately sinking ankle deep in the mud. His emotions have been suppressed for days but the mud on his boots is the final straw. He walks back onto the porch

and starts to clean his left boot on the pants leg
of the drifter who had insulted the Chief. Both
men immediately realize they are looking into
the eyes of pure hell. They want no part of this
man. "Sorry, mister, didn't mean anything..." the
man with one dirty pants leg says as both men
hurriedly walk away.

Ocher looks around and sees the Sheriff, "I
guess I'm not as intimidating as I thought."

The Sheriff's shakes his head, "Come on in.
You're all welcome."

"Sherriff Walsenburg, this is my good friend
Red Bluff."

"Call me George," he says, as he extends his
hand to the Chief. "You keep mighty
troublesome company in that one," nodding
toward Ocher with a smile. "He moseys into
town with some of the most dangerous men in
the territory in tow carrying over $50,000 in
cash, stops an assassination and then backs
down two of the of the roughest characters
around. In addition, come to find out, he's a
compadre of Abel Jones. Good man to call a
friend."

"Yes, he is," Red Bluff replies.

"Not to be impolite but I have to keep peace
around here. When are you headed out with
Abel?"

"Is there are problem?" Ocher asks.

"Not a problem. But the townsfolk are
avoiding the north end of town. Red Bluff has
posted an honor guard around the undertakers

place with some of the meanest looking braves all decked out. You talk about intimidating."

"We will leave at first light. Ok?" Ocher asks.

"Fine by me. I'll go and get the money and bring it to the funeral parlor. Got a feeling nobody gonna try and take it from you with all of those braves around. You're all welcome to stay out at the cabin if you want, but the undertaker has rooms for you. Be better for an early start if you stay here in town, at least for me. He also has a wagon for you."

"Thanks, George. We'll head up to the undertakers and be gone by dawn."

"Thanks, and be safe."

Chapter Twenty-Three

It's easy to find the undertaker, there isn't a soul around for blocks. The scene is somber and eerie at the same time. The honor guard is indeed intimidating or would be if Ocher didn't know them already

Ocher walks through the double doors of stained glass into a dark parlor. A squat, obese man steps out of a side door and in a high squeaky voice asks, "How may I assist you?"

Ocher almost laughs at the comical sight and voice of the man. "I am a friend of Abel Jones."

"Good, my business is suffering from those savages outside. When can you leave?" the squeaky man asks.

"At first light. The men outside are not savages but my friends. You best remember that, little man," Ocher responds.

Taken aback, the fat man responds., "There are still several hours of daylight and I can have

Mr. Jones moved into the wagon. It would be best if you left now."

"All right, best be shed of this horrid place anyway. How much do I owe you for your services?" Ocher asks.

"Your account is current. Please take your friends with you. Come around back into the memory garden. The wagon and Mr. Jones will be there. Good day." The little man turns on his left heel and waddles away.

Ocher just shakes his head and exits through the stained glass doors. "We are leaving now, best for all concerned." Red Bluff grunts his yes grunt.

"Thank you, Red Bluff. You are a true friend and a great warrior," Ocher says, offering his hand.

Red Bluff accepts the hand. He grunts acknowledging the comment. "We go to our winter camp. You will have safe passage through all nations. Jones was an honored warrior and friend." With no further ceremony the braves mount up and leave, taking the quickest path away of town.

Stacey, Austin, Vernon and the Sheriff are waiting by a wagon.

"I put the saddle bags under the seat," Stacey whispers.

Without even a word, a man hands the reins of the team hitched to the wagon to Ocher and walks away. Ocher wraps the reins around the hand brake and walks to the rear of the wagon. Abel Jones is lying in an open coffin wrapped in the most beautiful white tanned deer hide, adorned with stunning beaded work.

Ocher looks around at Stacey, Austin and Vernon.

Stacey walks over next to Ocher, "Those body wrappings are for the most honored. All Nations will recognize that. We will not be bothered during the journey. Red Bluff explained that to us earlier."

Ocher nods his head in agreement. "But what about supplies?"

Stacey just smiles, "We arranged a cache of supplies. We will be there by sunset."

Ocher strokes the muzzle of the Pinto, "Time to take Abel home." He steps up into the wagon, unwraps the reins, says "Yaw," then snaps the reins. Sad about the mission but happy that Stacey is with him. As well as the kids.

The travel is comfortable between Ocher and Stacey. Ocher reveals all to Stacey, now that there are no secrets between them.

The Pinto acts as a forward guard accompanied by Austin and Vernon. Ocher and Stacey watch as they gallop by only slowing down their adventures when the caravan stops for the evening.

The inclement weather follows them. Just as they arrive at Clovis and Elizabeth Narvones' ranch, the snow begins with a flurry and does not stop for two days.

When they depart there are snowmen almost everywhere. Austin and Vernon are finally getting to act like kids again. The sadness surrounding the caravan is slowly beginning to melt like the snow.

Ocher leaves five hundred dollars with Clovis only after a heated discussion. "This is your part of the reward money," Ocher finally convinces Clovis.

Chapter Twenty-Four

Ocher enjoys riding next to Stacey and watching Austin, Vernon and the Pinto ride through the country side without a care.

At noon, the first day after leaving the Narvone ranch, the caravan stops.

"Aren't you worried about those three running around? This is pretty wild country," Stacey asks.

"Nope," Ocher responds, pointing toward a small group of rocks pillared up. "We have company. I guess they're kind of an honor guard. I've seen several of those since we left this morning. They are just keeping out of sight."

"Apache?" Stacey asks, putting the coffee pot on to boil and unwrapping biscuits with bacon.

"That would be my guess. Red Bluff said that all nations respected Abel. And we are headed straight into Apache Land. Last I knew this was Chief Stone Face's Territory."

"You know him?" Stacey asks, pouring coffee.

"No. Just heard of him."

The three wild ones return to camp for a bit of rest and food before continuing their exploration of the countryside.

"Uncle Ocher," Austin begins, "Are there Indians around here?"

"Why do you ask?"

"We thought we saw someone on a pony. We went over there and saw a hoof print. It didn't seem to have a horseshoe."

Ocher looks at the two, "Yes, there are Indians around. Don't be afraid. They are kind of looking out after us. Ok?"

"Because of Mr. Jones?" Vernon asks.

"Yes."

The caravan continues on south. The further they go the warmer it becomes. "Sure glad to be shed of that snow and freezing rain," Ocher says one evening. "It's not quite as hot as I like, but sure better than cold."

"Don't get much snow in the jungle?" Stacey asks, grinning at Ocher.

"Don't recall much of it. Back there in the mountains was my first time. Don't care for it."

"Good snuggling weather," Stacey says.

Ocher doesn't know how to respond, "Need to check on the wagon and horses."

Day after day the honor guard begins to reveal itself. They don't come into camp and they avoid Austin and Vernon. On the evening of the sixth day a dozen ornately dressed Indians ride into camp.

What appears to be the oldest of the group rides forward. "Taza send us to bring Abel Jones to camp. We leave when sun returns."

The group form a circle around the camp, but remain mounted.

Stacey looks at Ocher, "Taza?"

"Yep. No use asking about Stone Face. They won't say much about the dead."

"They gonna sit like that all night?"

"I reckon so. Maybe some others will come in at night and change up with them. I don't really know."

"Should we be scared, Uncle Ocher?" Vernon asks. Austin, nodding, wants to know as well.

"No. If they wanted to harm us, they had days to do it. We're fine."

Even with Ocher's assurance, no one sleeps, including Ocher.

By dawn, the escorted caravan heads south, Austin, Vernon and the Pinto close in by the wagon.

The day proceeds uneventful, almost. More *escorts* arrive by the hour. Ocher recognizes many of the braves. Some Apaches are from White Elk's camp. Many of the them shared the adventure of retrieving the horses that had been stolen from Ocher by the bandit Chavez.

The surprise is Blue Sand, a Navajo, with several warriors from Three Toe Bear's camp.

Ocher is carrying the obsidian knife he took from Blue Sand. *My mistake*, Ocher thinks. *I can remedy that error, hopefully.*

MIKE GIPSON

Navajo, Ute, Arapaho and Apache honor guards. Not something one sees every day.

At mid-afternoon the party arrives at camp.

The size of the camp is enormous. There are lodge fires as far as the eye can see. The escorts lead the wagon through the heart of the teepees, the men regaling Abel with war cries, the women wailing and the children looking about bewildered.

They arrive at what Ocher knows is the ceremonial fire: a very large open space with a larger than normal fire ring. The lodges adjacent to the area are festooned with bead work, gourds and draped feathered pieces. Blue Sand is standing in front of the most decorative of the lodges.

"You are welcome here, Ocher Jones, now and always," Taza says.

"Thank you, Chief Taza. My lodge will be your lodge. Now and forever," Ocher responds.

Geronimo steps forward and grunts his approval. He continues toward Stacey and holds out his hand. Stacey takes it. Vernon and Austin stare wide-eyed at the medicine man.

Geronimo stares into Stacey's face and then turns to Ocher. " '*Ni' naki.*"

Ocher does not know the meaning of the phase. Taza steps forward, "Life couple."

Stacey just smiles. Austin giggles. Ocher nods.

Taza smiles at Ocher and points to several teepees. "You and the *indee,* adult male, there," he orders, giving Vernon the compliment of being a grown up. "You and the young squaw will be there," he says to Stacey, indicating another teepee.

The wagon has been surrounded by twelve Apache braves dressed in tanned deer skins with bead work. Two of the twelve have taken the leads for the horses and are leading the wagon away. Ocher looks for the other tribes' representatives, but they're nowhere to be seen.

"His spirit will be presented to the owl at sunset. Then we will celebrate his life," Taza says and turns away followed by Geronimo.

Immediately the matriarch squaws surround Stacy and Austin and lead them away, leaving Ocher and Vernon standing with the traveling kits of the party. Ocher picks up Stacey and Austin's kits to take them to the teepee and is cut off by one of the squaws. She relieves him of the bags and waddles away.

"We are over there," Ocher says, seeing that Vernon is as bewildered as he is.

Chapter Twenty-Five

Ocher and Vernon clean up as best they can and attire themselves in the best they have. They look like street beggars compared to the Apache braves.

Just before sunset a detail of braves from all the Nations arrive, including Blue Sand, to escort Ocher and Vernon to the resting place of Abel Jones. They are joined by the Squaw Guard escorting Stacey and Austin. They're not dressed as street beggars.

Stacey is dressed in a tanned deer skin skirt, festooned like the *Sailing Vessel Anne Belle,* but instead of flags and pennants it's feathers and beads. Breathtaking. The hand-woven shawl draped over her shoulders is multi-colored, hiding whatever is underneath.

Austin steps out from behind Stacey and Vernon stops dead in his tracks, right behind Ocher, who has already stopped. She is a stunning young lady. Every young Apache boy is also paying attention. Both women are stunning and they know it, and smile at *the boys.*

The two groups intermingle, and, as they start the procession, a chant begins and continues until they arrive at Abel's resting place.

A very large slab rock has been levered up and being held in place by ropes. Abel's body has been laid under the slab in a depression. Around him are gourds filled with water and spices for his journey. Desert flowers are covering most of Abel's lower body. On the under side of the slab are paintings of scenes depicting what Ocher assumes are adventures that Abel has shared with those gathered.

Geronimo steps forward and speaks in Apache until the sun is gone. Finally, ending his speech, he turns to Ocher. "We return to camp and celebrate his spirit. This camp's medicine man will stay here to await the Owl spirit." Geronimo turns and starts back toward camp.

Geronimo and Taza sit side by side with their backs to the sunset facing the east. Ocher and Vernon are on Geronimo's right and Stacy and Austin are on Taza's left.

Food and water are served in bowls and the stories begin. Hours upon hours of stories about Abel and the Apaches he traveled with over the years are told, some stories in English but most in Apache.

Sometime in the pre-dawn the camp's medicine man comes into the camp firelight and speaks to Geronimo. He holds up his hand and all is silent. "The owl has taken our friend and warrior's spirit." The story telling stops and the dancing begins.

Ocher watches the dancing and gets the rhythm of the dancers and then asks Stacey to join him. Vernon and Austin are already stomping around, Vernon keeping the other young boys at bay.

After several trips around the camp fire Stacey says, "My guardians have said it's all right to walk together, with a chaperone."

Ocher smiles, "We have been marooned, shot at and on the trail together for a while. Chaperone?"

"Yes, Ocher Jones, chaperone."

"Well, then let us walk together, with a chaperone."

"Chaperone might be the wrong word. Look." Just outside the circle of their conversation stands what appears to be half of the squaws in camp, all smiling.

Ocher drops his head and shakes it, reaching for her hand. The hiss from the surrounding contingent would indicate *no hand holding.*

Stacey laughs, "Miss Barrington's finishing school has nothing on these ladies."

They walk just outside of the camp, the half-moon well up in the sky. Ocher stops and turns to Stacey. The audience moves in closer, "As I said earlier, we have shared quite a bit of adventure. And you know about me, my past and what I was trained to be."

"Yes, and I'm still here," she says, cutting him short.

"Well, that's what I want to talk about, well...I well... Stacey, well. I know I should ask your Pa but, well,"

"Get to the point, Ocher Jones."

"Will you marry me?"

"I have to," she replies.

"What?"

"Geronimo saw it, my folks have seen it, I've known it from the day you sat on our front porch when you brought Woody in. You're the only one that doesn't know. Of course I'll marry you."

"I mean now, here, tomorrow. I'll speak to Geronimo."

"He already knows by now. Look around. The guard detail has left. We're alone," Stacey reaches up and pulls Ocher's head down for their first kiss.

As quickly as the chaperones had disappeared, they reappear. Stacey is whisked away and Ocher is left standing in the moonlight. He ambles back to his teepee. Vernon is snoring quietly.

The camp reminds Ocher of a bee hive. Women, men and children are running about in what looks like complete turmoil. Ocher knows better. The frenzy is far from disorganized. The wedding is scheduled for sunset the day after tomorrow.

Ocher is measured, remeasured, draped in white deer skin, undraped and then redraped. Taza and Geronimo go through the ceremony. Somebody's wife checks with Stacey to insure that she gets the ceremony she wants. Austin is nowhere to be seen and Vernon and the other boys in camp are off running through the desert. The days go quickly.

A big meal is delivered around noon to Ocher's tent, accompanied by another briefing about the ceremony. His outfit is delivered. It fits perfectly. There's no other word for the white tanned deer skin suit, beautiful.

Taza arrives to escort Ocher to the ceremony. The whole camp is there standing around the central camp fire. All are dressed in their ceremonial attire. Vernon, dressed in deer skins, is standing off to the side waiting for Ocher to arrive.

The wedding teepee flap is opened and out steps Stacey, also dressed in a white deer skin dress and blouse. She is stunning. She arrives escorted by Taza's senior wife. Stacey stands next to Ocher. Austin stands next to Vernon dressed in tanned deer skins.

Geronimo arrives and faces Ocher and Stacey. A grizzled old woman hands Geronimo a decorative bowl filled with what smells of burning sage. Geronimo passes the bowl over himself, Ocher and Stacey.

Taza, standing just off to the side, says, "The smoke will cleanse you and send your prayers to the Creator."

Geronimo hands the bowl back to the old woman. She hands him a length of deer skin cut into a strip and decorated in the clan's colors.

Ocher and Stacey present their right hands as they were briefed to do. Geronimo binds their hands together, "Now this couple will be seen as one."

Ocher turns to face Stacey and she faces him. Together they speak,

"Now you will feel no rain
for each of us will shelter the other.
Now you will feel no cold,
for we will be warmth to the other.
Now there will be no loneliness,
for we will be companions to the other.
Now we are two persons,
but there is only one life before us,
May beauty surround us both in the
the journey ahead and through the years,
May happiness be our companion and our
days together be good and long upon the
earth."

The squaws in camp start to sing and apparently every warrior must slap Ocher on the back. The sun is just setting and the dancing begins. Ocher stands with Stacey, she just in front of him, as they are still bound by their right hands. They manage to stay and watch the dancing for about two hours before *sneaking* off to the wedding tent to untie the binding.

Sometime during the night the dancing and celebration end and things quiet down.

Just after dawn Ocher and Stacey decide to leave the teepee. As they emerge the whole camp is quietly sitting and watching the wedding teepee. When Ocher steps out with Stacey the camp erupts. The squaws start singing and the braves start slapping Ocher on the back.

It's a day of transition. By noon the camp has reduced by half. The teepees are razed and clan by clan leave. With no ceremony Geronimo leaves, but not before stopping to place a blessing on Ocher and Stacey.

"Treat yourselves and each other with respect, and remind yourselves often of what brought you together."

Then he mounts a pale pony and is gone.

Chief Taza and several braves bring the wagon to the wedding teepee, "Our clan will leave tomorrow. There will be no Apache camp here again. It is a sacred place. All of the Nations, friend and enemy will mourn him."

"Yes, Chief, I will miss him very much," Ocher responds.

"You will carry him here," Taza says pointing to his chest.

"I will."

"So will I," Stacey adds.

"You have honored the Apache by sharing your binding ceremony with us. Geronimo has made you his blood brother. Now you are a part of the Apache Nation. The little ones as well. You will travel through Apache Land safely, always."

Like Geronimo, he turns and leaves.

Ocher has one more duty to perform. He knows where Blue Sand is camped and can see that he and the Navajo Braves are preparing to depart. He walks over to Blue Sand.

"Blue Sand, at another time I was foolish. I thought my honor was more important than yours. I dishonored myself by taking this," Ocher holds out the black obsidian knife he took from Blue Sand.

Blue Sand just looks at the knife.

"This knife is Navajo, it's spirit is Navajo. It belongs with a warrior and Chief of the Navajo," Ocher hands the knife to Blue Sand.

"You honor me, *Nd'e' Sdzan*. You taught me much that day. Pride is not honor. A Chief must lead with honor and leave pride for others. You forced pride from me, thank you. The knife, please keep it. It is with a warrior, a chief, a brother Navajo." Blue Sand turns and strides away.

"Taza calls this place a sacred place. Is that because of Abel?" Stacey asks. "It's breathtaking, looks like somebody painted the desert."

"Abel told me that it's been a sacred place since the ancient days. Yes, it's breathtaking and also deadly. If you don't know where water and shelter are in this place, well, you'll die in a beautiful place," Ocher says as he cinches up his saddle."

"What about the curse, Uncle Ocher?" Vernon inquires, already knowing the answer.

"Curse?" Austin asked.

"Yes, curse. The stone trees," Ocher starts. "The stone trees that are here have been here even before the ancient ones. It's unknown why they are here. If you take a piece of a tree, it's said that it will be recovered and returned here."

"How," Austin asks, reaching into her pocket taking out a small piece of stone tree.

"In some of the nations they are called skin walkers or shape shifters. They'll find whoever steals from this sacred place and take what was stolen. The thief is punished in many horrible ways." Ocher continues the telling.

"I didn't know, Uncle Ocher," Austin says, almost in tears holding out her hand with a small piece of a stone tree.

"It's ok, Austin. Just leave it here. You'll be fine."

Austin walks away from the small caravan and places the piece of stone tree near a larger piece. The ground changing color as her tears fall in the sand. She whispers, "I'm sorry," as she returns back to the wagon.

Stacey takes Ocher's hand, "I want to go home."

"Me too, now that I have a home."

Chapter Twenty-Six

"**S**omething wrong Mr. Jones?"

"Yes, Mrs. Jones"

"What?"

"I have no idea how to speak to your mom and dad about all of this."

"Amazing, you are truly amazing. You have faced down pirates, the Apache Nation, bandits and assassins. After all of that, you're afraid of my dad?"

"Yes."

"Does my father trust you?"

"I hope so."

"You don't know?"

"I, well, I don't know. I suppose so."

"Do you think my folks would have let me go all the way to Colorado to be with you if they didn't trust you?"

"I guess so."

Before Ocher can answer Vernon rides up, Austin right behind. "Uncle Ocher, I'm getting kinda hungry. Can we stop soon?"

"Not yet, Vernon. Soon. Have to find the right spot and we'll stop for the night."

"Me and Vernon can scout ahead for a good place," Austin says, siding up next to Vernon.

"No need to scout about."

"Why? Do you know a place?"

"You two haven't been paying attention," Stacey says smiling. "Look over there," She says pointing. "See those rocks stacked up?"

Both of the youngsters turn and look, seeing three small rocks stacked up.

"Who stacked those up?" Austin asks.

"I would say that Taza has some braves out ahead of us leaving a trail. They will leave two stacks of rocks showing a direction to go for a night camp. You two go on ahead and see if you can spot the sign," Stacey says, giving a dismissal wave of her hand.

The kids turn the horses from the wagon and gallop up the trail.

"Well, Mrs. Jones. You're turning out to be pretty trail wise. I didn't know you saw those markers."

"Dad taught me. He can read sign with the best of them. Not only on the trail, but with people too. Don't worry about talking to him. I think he read the sign about us a long time ago. Mom too. Look," Stacey says, pointing up the trail.

Vernon is in the middle of the trail waving his hat and pointing. Off to the south Austin is doing the same.

"Guess they found the marker, "Ocher observes.

Stacey nods, "Good, I'm getting hungry too."

The camp is perfect. Water source, sheltered from the wind, and someone has already gathered wood for a fire.

Ocher and Stacey rummage through the baskets that Taza's' people placed in the back of the wagon. There's enough food to last, well, a long time. They settle on prairie grouse, roasted prickly pear, dried fruit and cold spring water.

They are all sitting around the fire, watching the sunset, with coffee on the fire. Ocher has never imagined this when he left the Philippines. His reality at the time was a skilled merchant of death, a loner, a deserter of sorts, with only the hope of a life not guided by his past. Now, here, with Stacey, he has a future, a home and perhaps a family. He reaches over and takes Stacey's hand.

Chapter Twenty-Seven

The days go comfortably by, especially since the caravan doesn't have to look for water or camp sites. They just have to follow the sign.

Just before noon on the sixth day Vernon and Austin come riding back to the wagon.

"Uncle Ocher," Vernon says, pointing toward the dust cloud east of their path.

"Who could that be?" Austin asks.

"Sure isn't our friends. They wouldn't need to make themselves known that way. We'll just have to wait and see," Ocher replies. "Stay close in until we find out who."

"Ok," both kids reply.

The dust cloud gets closer and reveals the source: a Cavalry patrol, without a scout.

The troop rides in close, the man in the lead coming up to the wagon after giving a hand signal for the rest to stay put.

Without preamble, "What are you folks doing out here? This is Apache Territory. If those savages find you, they will show you no mercy."

"Who might you be?" Ocher asks.

"Lieutenant Dexter Ambrose, class of '68 commanding B Troop, Fort Sill, Oklahoma. We are here to take Geronimo in custody for questioning."

"Good luck, Lieutenant. If you'd order your troop off the trail, we'll be on our way," Ocher states, having decided he doesn't like Dexter Ambrose, class of '68.

"I don't make a habit of repeating myself. However, what are you folks doing out here?"

"Well, Mr. Ambrose," Ocher starts to respond.

"Lieutenant Ambrose."

"Dexter," Ocher begins again, "Have those men move off the trail."

The Lieutenant understands he has just been insulted in front of his men. He spurs his horse toward the back of the wagon. "I'll just have a look in the wagon. There are gun runners about."

Austin moves her horse between the wagon and the Lieutenant so he can not look in the wagon.

Dexter Ambrose starts to reach out and grab the reins of Austin's horse to move her out of the way.

Several things happen at once. Vernon, who had taken up a position on the opposite side of the wagon, jumps out of the saddle and starts across the back of the wagon to confront the Lieutenant.

Ocher is slightly ahead of Vernon after leaving his seat at the front of the wagon. His destination is also the Lieutenant.

Austin, taking the situation in stride, has retrieved her boot knife and has it right under the Cavalry officer's chin.

But it's the arrow striking the side of the wagon that brings everything to a halt.

Ocher and Vernon stop their advance.

The men of B Troop haven't made any attempt to back up the Lieutenant.

"Dexter, you and your men need to leave. I would suggest all the way back to Oklahoma. Austin, ease up," Ocher says from the bed of the wagon.

Austin just nods and puts her boot knife back.

Trying to regain some dignity, the lieutenant says, "You are under arrest for assault of a U.S Army Officer."

"You want that whole troop over there to testify you were bested by an eleven year old girl?" Ocher asks grinning. "You think that's just one lone brave out there with a bow and arrow?"

Austin spurs her horse forward into the officer's horse to emphasize the point.

"Lieutenant, you have no business being out here. You and your troop will die out here. I can see from the condition of your men and the horses, you are short on water. I suspect you are just as short on food. Even if you find Geronimo, and you won't, you intend to take on the whole Apache Nation with them?"

"I will find Geronimo. I was number one in my class in tactics, and that savage is not equal to my intelligence."

"True, Dexter. Out here he is smarter than you," Ocher offers. "The desert has provided the Apache for centuries. Food, water and shelter. This is his home. The only thing the desert will provide you is a slow death. You and that rag tag bunch over there."

"This isn't over. I will prevail."

"No, you won't. Those savages out there," Ocher points in the direction the arrow originated, "as you call them, will lead you around out here until you die. They obviously know where you are, but you have no idea where they are. Go home, Dexter."

Lieutenant Dexter Ambrose, class of '68, commanding troop B, turns his horse North, in the direction of an unknown party of Apaches, "Forward Ho."

"What a foolish man," Stacey says. "He'll lead all of those men to their death and never see one Apache."

"Yep, unfortunately there are a whole lot more just like him that will die out here," Ocher observes sitting back down in the wagon seat.

"Think he will see the rock markers, Uncle Ocher?" Vernon asks, stepping out of the wagon and back in the saddle.

"No, he don't seem to be very trail wise."

Austin is staring at Vernon.

"What?" he asks.

"You were going to protect me."

"Of course."

Chapter Twenty-Eight

"**W**ell, Mrs. Jones, today's the day," Ocher says stepping up into the wagon.

"You still fretting over facing my dad?"

"Yes."

"Don't. Just don't let those two get out ahead us. They'll get to dad before you get a chance," Stacey remarks, looking toward Austin and Vernon.

"Yep, as trail wise as they have become, they're still kids."

The caravan does not stop for a nooning. They all agree they want to get home. Ocher tells Vernon and Austin to stay close in to the wagon. They are confused by the order but comply.

"We got company," Ocher says, pointing out two figures highlighted on the ridge east of the trail.

"One of them is headed this way," Stacey adds.

Jonathan, the oldest of the remaining boys still at home with Ollie and Marta, rides up to the wagon. "Howdy," he says, removing his hat and tipping it toward Stacey.

"Howdy, John. What are grinning about?" Ocher asks.

"Nothing, Uncle Ocher, nothing."

"Why were you were up there watching the trail?" Ocher asks, suspecting some chicanery.

"Because, Uncle Ocher."

"Jonathon, what's going on?"

"Can't say. I can tell you that Mr. Livingston wants to talk to you. Vernon, PaPa Ollie, well you can guess."

Ocher notes that Jonathon does not look or speak to Austin. Stacey reaches over and places her hand on Ocher's shoulder. She whispers, "Something is wrong."

Ocher nods slightly.

"James went on ahead. By the time we get to the Livingston's everybody will be there... for supper."

The ride to the Double LL is silent. *'Mr. Livingston wants to talk to you'* is running through Ocher's mind.

Even at a distance Ocher can see the whole tribe of Livingstons, Von Derrs and all of the hands standing around the yard outside the kitchen. The big table is set up and loaded with food.

Ocher stops the wagon, steps down and helps Stacey down. Vernon and Austin dismount. They join Ocher and Stacey.

Lewis Livingston isn't smiling. Neither is Ollie. Amanda and Marta aren't either.

Ocher gathers his courage, takes a first step toward Mr. Livingston and then makes the walk.

Lewis stands rock steady, arms folded across his chest. He's still not smiling.

Ocher stops at arm's length in front of Lewis, "Mr. Livingston," he starts.

"Jones," Livingston starts uncrossing his arms, still not smiling. "Congratulations, son, welcome to the family." Lewis puts out his hand for a handshake but grabs Ocher in a big hug instead.

The rest of the family erupts. Amanda and Marta rush forward. The kids run to Ocher, then to Stacey then to Vernon, then to Austin and back to Ocher. The ranch hands weave their way through the pandemonium to shake Ocher's hand.

"How in the world did you know?" Ocher finally gets the opportunity to ask.

Lewis just points. There on the chair where Stacey usually sits is a very colorful hand woven blanket.

'That was draped across the hitching rail at the front of the house a couple of days ago. We been out here long enough to know that is a wedding blanket. Sometimes used during a wedding ceremony and kept at the foot of the couple's bed, for life. Who else could it have been?" Amanda gushes.

As the elation dies down a bit, Lewis and Ollie approach Ocher, "We need to talk, privately," Lewis says to Ocher, nodding toward the house.

"Ok."

Lewis, Ollie and Ocher sit down in the kitchen, alone. "I'll cut right to it," Lewis starts. "The Peterson woman up and left."

"Without Austin?" Ocher responds.

"Yep. She came over here wanting to sell the ranch. They owned the place outright. It was reasonable, so well, Ollie bought her ranch."

"Ollie bought it?" Ocher looks at Ollie, a confused look on his face.

Lewis continues, "Yep. Marta wants the place rebuilt along with a school."

"A school?" Ocher asks.

"We'll get to that. After getting her money she and her daughter up and left. No note, no nothing. She left Austin high and dry. Well, not quite," Lewis finishes.

"Me and Marta always took in boys. Marta wants to adopt Austin," Ollie says, a big smile on his face. "Up to her."

"A school?" Ocher repeats.

"A school. For boys and girls. What Marta wants....well," Ollie answers with a smile

Ocher looks at Lewis then Ollie and stands, "First things first. Let's ask Austin what she wants."

Ocher walks to the kitchen door and sees Marta standing next to Austin in anticipation. Ocher smiles and nods toward the pair. Marta leans down and says something to Austin and takes her hand.

"Sit down, Austin," Ocher says. "We have to talk."

"Something's wrong, isn't it, Uncle Ocher?"

"Yes, but we can fix it. No easy way to say this, Austin. Mrs. Peterson sold the ranch and left. She left without you."

"Oh," is Austin's only comment.

Marta can't keep her excitement in check, "Austin, I, we...want you to come and live with us and become part of our family."

"Adopt me?"

"Yes, but that's up to you," Marta continues.

"You mean I can stay here, with Vernon, I mean all of you? Uncle Ocher and Aunt Stacey, forever?"

"If you want," Ollie answers.

"Wait, aren't you going back to San Francisco?"

"No, Austin. We bought the Peterson place. We are going to rebuild it and stay here. That ok with you?" Ollie answers.

"Oh, yes! The Petersons just took me in. I wasn't really in their family. I was just there. Now, a real family. Can we tell everybody? Right now?"

Chapter Twenty-Nine

The congratulations, revelry and exuberance finally mellow out and the logistics of living take over.

Ocher and Stacey - Mr. and Mrs. Jones - move into their own home, the Concho Ranch, the younger boys in the bunk house.

The Livingstons and the older boys are at the Double LL. Ollie and Marta are taking up residence in their temporary cabin at the newly acquired ranch with Austin.

Evening meals are at the "big table."

At supper one evening, "I can't ride a horse that far. Don't believe the horse would like it much either," Ollie says.

"Taking a wagon to San Francisco makes taking supplies a might easier," Lewis adds.

"That's what I figured," Ollie responds. "Jeremy sold the place out there and crated up all of the stuff Marta and me want. Just couldn't get nobody to bring it here across the desert. Especially through Apache or Arapaho territory."

"Apache territory won't be a problem for us," Ocher observes. "Hope the same holds true for the Arapaho. We'll be well south of the Navajo and Hopi lands."

"Still, it's gonna be hot and thirsty. But that holds true for most of the year," Ollie concludes. "By the time we get back, those adobe bricks will be weathered and dry. The boys can get started on the house and school. Have us a proper place soon."

Ocher doesn't say much about the trip.

Stacey and Amanda have already decided who will go and who will stay before Ollie has been allowed any input.

Ocher and Stacey will lead in a wagon. Ollie and Butch, the third oldest at home, will be in the second wagon. Jimmy, next in line behind Butch, will ride but teamster a wagon back east. Vernon and Austin will wrangle the extra horses. Better to have them along than have them sneaking off and trailing the wagon train.

Jonathon, the oldest at home, will see to the adobe making. Marta will just be in charge.

After the travel has been decided, Ocher and Stacey ride out into the Apache Nation, make camp and wait.

"Evening, Other Hand," the Apache Brave entering the camp is left handed. "You are all welcome here," Ocher says, using his limited Apache.

Other Hand and four other braves enter the camp, *"Nd'e' Sdzan,* you are welcome in our nation," Other Hand replies.

Ocher knows it is impolite to get right to the heart of his question without exchanging pleasantries or to ask the meaning of *Nd'e' Sdzan*. The next half hour is spent on the weather, hunting and family. To Ocher and Stacey's surprise she is invited into the exchange.

Finally, Ocher gets to business. "Other Hand, our family has need to cross the Apache Nation traveling to the setting sun and return. We would not do this without permission from the Chiefs of the Nation."

Other Hand grunts, nods, "I will bring your notion to the council."

"Thank you, Other Hand." Before Ocher can say anything else or ask about the *Nd'e' Sdzan*, Other Hand and the braves are gone.

"That couldn't mean anything bad or he wouldn't have agreed to ask the council, " Stacey observes.

"Hope so."

Two days later as Ocher steps out onto the front porch of the ranch house there is a pile of three stones on the porch.

From behind Ocher, "Looks like we have permission," Stacey says.

"Would seem so."

Chapter Thirty

If someone wanted to raid the ranches, today would be the day. The day of departure.

The Livingstons, Van Derrs, kids and hands all ride out with the departing group.

"We'll ride out with you for a while, just to make sure you get started in the right direction," Lewis says jokingly. "Amanda wants to ride a long with Stacey for a bit."

Ocher knows Lewis wants to ride along with his daughter just as much as her mom does.

At mid-morning the parade stops at the rim of a long east-west canyon. Hugs and tears are exchanged and the wagons and outriders head west. Those left behind sit and watch until the wagons are mere dots in the distance.

At the nooning of the first day, Ollie remarks, "Jeremy moving those crates down to Los Angles is sure going to save us a lot of time. And a lot of desert."

"Yep," Ocher responds. "Due west almost in a straight line. Most of it through Apache

Territory. Although a ride from Los Angles to Frisco along the coast might not be too bad."

"An extra six weeks," Ollie says. "Used to make that trip. Ain't all that glorious. I want to get back and get on with it. Already missing Marta and the boys."

"You saying you don't want to travel along with me and Austin, Mr. Van Derr?" Stacey adds, looking up at Ollie, her hands on her hips and a big smile.

"Where are those two, anyway?" Ollie answers.

"Yonder, watering the horses," Ocher points with his coffee cup.

After changing out the wagon teams, drinking their fill of fresh spring water, they continue west.

"Sure a whole lot easier traveling when someone is guiding for you," Ocher remarks, turning the lead wagon south after seeing the stone marker.

Ollie trails along, followed by the rest of the caravan.

"Couldn't be a better place to stop," Ollie says, stepping down from his wagon. "Well, maybe if it had a dining room. But sure will do."

There's no need to assign duties. The whole bunch are trail wise. They know what needs to be done and they just do it.

The horses get picketed, the Pinto taking up guard duty over the mares. Ocher gathers fire wood, Ollie takes out the fixings for supper and gets it started. Butch waters the horses with Austin and Vernon's help. Then they fill the water barrels. Jimmy finishes the cooking. Super is served just as the sun sets.

"I know there ain't a tenderfoot among us, but, that was an easy day. Best enjoy them whilst we can. There's gonna be some real tough ones ahead. Guide rocks or no," Ollie remarks to no one in particular.

"Yea, but won't it be a tale to tell, PaPa Ollie," Austin remarks smiling, calling Ollie PaPa.

"Don't believe we need a night watch. In fact I imagine there are a couple of friendly folks out there taking care of that," Ocher says, standing, as he heads for the space where Stacey laid out their bedrolls.

"They're almost as good as you are, Uncle Ocher," Vernon says.

"Almost," Ocher says smiling. "Almost."

Ocher is the first one up and discovers the decorative war lance stuck in the ground in the middle of camp. *Must have taken offense about being better than they are. Might have to rethink that.* He starts coffee.

"Wow, Uncle Ocher, a war lance. What's it mean?" Vernon asks excitedly.

"Just giving us permission to cross Apache Territory. Those far west camps don't know as well as those around here," Ocher explains, holding the lance. "We'll wrap it up and keep it hid until we need it."

"Why hide it?" Austin asks.

"If we come across that Army officer, Dexter Ambrose. He might get the wrong idea and just tag along with us. Thinking maybe we would lead him to Geronimo," Stacey offers.

"Yep," Ocher agrees. Not adding anything about being sneaked up on.

The days become routine if not monotonous. Ride, stop, change horses, deal with watering horses and people. Stop, water, eat, sleep. Not much in a change of scenery either.

One nooning a dust cloud appears north of the spring where the caravan stops and is brewing coffee.

"Got to be that Dexter fella," Ocher remarks. "He's got to announce to everybody and everything he's coming."

Sure enough, out of the dust cloud Troop B arrive and without preamble Dexter dismounts and gives orders to his men.

Ollie, sitting on a rock with a cup of coffee in his hand, "Dexter, out here we do cotton to some bit of politeness. A fella don't just ride up and step down without gettin' invited. Water hole or not. We will gladly share, but it just ain't polite to get too pushy."

Lieutenant Dexter Ambrose, commanding Cavalry Troop B, starts to take a step forward in an effort to intimidate a sitting Ollie.

Ollie stands. Dexter takes a step back. Ollie beacons to Austin, "You've met my daughter I believe?"

Dexter is completely unnerved. A smiling Troop B just stays mounted.

"My apologies, Sir, Miss. We have been pursuing the savage Geronimo and are tired, thirsty and hungry. I, we, would be grateful if you would allow us access and use of the water hole."

"Sure," Austin says. "It'd be wise to look after them horses first. They look done in."

"Yes, that would be prudent as we are closing in on Geronimo," the Lieutenant remarks.

"I doubt you are within a hundred miles of Geronimo, Lieutenant," Ocher states, as he sides up along Ollie. "If I was you, I would set up camp here for a couple of days. As Austin said, your horses need rest and so do those men. There are rabbit, prairie hens about and a deer or two if you're a good shot. Geronimo isn't going anywhere. In your condition you really don't want to find him."

Dexter starts to argue.

"Best listen to the man," Butch says. Jimmy nods standing alongside.

Lieutenant Dexter Ambrose, Class of '68, takes stock of his situation. His men and horses look whipped to a frazzle. Yet the men and women standing in front of him look fresh, clean, well fed and are standing in the middle of the Apache Nation unafraid. "Company B dismount, make camp."

"Lieutenant, we'll be on our way. Good luck," Ocher says as he and the rest of his party turn and prepare to leave.

Vernon rides up alongside the wagon. "Uncle Ocher, why didn't you tell that Army man that he was chasing around in the Arapaho Nation?"

Ocher just smile, "I figured it is much safer than actually running into Geronimo or the Apaches."

"But the Arapahos?"

"They'll be moving toward their summer places, more north. The Lieutenant can run around in the sand and tumbleweeds and have it all pretty much to himself."

Vernon laughs and moves back toward the extra horses and Austin.

With every turn of the wagon wheels they get closer to California. There is water, and food but no respite from the heat, grit and boredom. The scenery doesn't change much.

"Seen one tumbleweed, you, well the rest don't change much," Ocher says, picking up the coffee pot. "The sunsets are something to see, but even I'm getting a bit tired of them. Be glad to get there."

The conversation kind of dies.

Finally, "You're getting to be a real mighty fine teamster, Stacey," Ollie notes, holding out his cup toward Ocher.

"I'll stick to ranching. At least with those horses you get to see the other end occasionally," Stacey replies.

"How much further, PaPa Ollie?" Austin jumps into the conversation.

"Ten days or so. We been taking care of the wagons and horses pretty well. Still, there could be a broke wheel or some other bother, but ten days."

Chapter Thirty -One

Some other bother arrives the next day just before nooning.

Austin and Vernon ride up from behind the wagons. "Uncle Ocher, riders coming in. It's Indians, but they don't appear to be Apache."

"But those are," Vernon says, pointing toward the southwest."

Ocher stops the wagon, reaches back and takes out the Apache War Lance and places it in the buggy whip stand on the side of the wagon. "No use running."

About a dozen or so Arapaho braves storm up to the lead wagon. After looking at the war lance and to the southwest at the arriving Apache party. "Give food, quick."

Ocher just glares at the speaking brave, "No."

"We take."

"No," Ocher stalls for time.

The Arapaho realizes that it's too late for them to run, so they wait.

Not a half an hour before the desert was empty, or appeared so, but now, over twenty

Indians, two wagons, horses, men, women are clustered in the heat and sand.

The Apache party ride in, unhurried, sitting tall and proud. Ocher does not recognize any of the warriors.

They spread out and the lead brave rides up to his counterpart of the Arapahos. In Spanish, "Your hunting grounds are there," pointing toward the north. "Is the game so poor you must come here and buzz around like the deer fly and pester Geronimo's blood brother?"

The Arapaho has been insulted and knows it. "Has Geronimo taken to protecting these weak and feeble white men?"

The Apache laughs, "Geronimo does not need to protect his brother, *Nd'e' Sdzan.*"

The Arapaho looks at Ocher then at the Apache party. Trying to save face, "It is a good day to die, but our women are hungry. We will let these white men live, for now." He turns and leads the other braves away, heading north.

Ocher sits and says nothing as does everyone else.

"*Nd'e' Sdzan*, I am Jlin-Litzque, you are welcome here."

"Thank you, Jlin-Litzque. What is the meaning of *Nd'e' Sdzan*?" Ocher asks.

The Apache hesitates, "It means *Two Spirits.*"

"Two Spirits?" Ocher asks.

Jlin-Litzque ponders on how to explain the meaning. Finally, he says, "This wolf has two sides. Which one you meet depends on you. It is the name Geronimo has given you."

"It is a great honor to be so named. Thank Geronimo when you see him," Ocher says as he replaces the war lance in the bed of the wagon. "There are Army men looking for him."

"Yes, we are watching them wander about in the desert. He is amused by them. Continue your journey straight into the western sun, *Nd'e Sdzan.*" Jlin-Litzque and the braves turn and disappear into the desert.

"*Nd'e' Sdzan*, Two Spirits. Geronimo certainly knows you, Mr. Jones," Stacey says, smiling at Ocher.

"That medicine man never ceases to amaze me. Due west," Ocher responds, waving his hand in a forward motion. Talking is for later.

Chapter Thirty-Two

Little by little civilization creeps closer to their trail: an abandoned wagon or parts of one, camp fires and glimpses of structures all appear.

At the nooning, Ollie points toward the sky, "Not far now. Seagulls. Probably by sundown."

"You mean a proper bath and clean sheets?" Stacey says as she smiles at Ollie.

"Last I was down here, they did have clean water and actually washed clothes," Ollie retorts.

"You been down this far?" Ocher asks.

"Yep. Used to teamster down here three or four times a year. More steady business going north from Frisco. But business is business."

"Seagulls?" Austin asks.

"See that white bird yonder?" Vernon points. "Used to see them all of the time when we lived up north," he tells her, assuming the mantle of a world traveler.

"Will I get to see the ocean?" Austin continues.

"Yes, Austin. I'll make sure you get to see the ocean." Ollie says, before Vernon has a chance to make the same offer.

"I've seen enough of the ocean for a while. I'll do something else that day," Stacey says.

Ollie takes the lead from the nooning and just before sunset the caravan pulls up in front of a large warehouse with *Stanley Shipping* stenciled on the side.

A tall gangling man is standing in the open doorway. He pushes himself off the door frame and limps toward the lead wagon, "Howdy, Ollie. Been expecting you."

"Howdy, Ned. Why the limp?" Ollie asks, stepping down from the wagon.

"Broke my leg a while back. Ain't healed right. Couldn't muscle cargo around too good. So's the old man made me the warehouse foreman."

"What day is it, Ned?" Stacey says in a weary voice.

"Thursday, Miss."

"No I mean, what month."

"Second week of September, I believe."

Stacey sits back a little and looks over at Ocher. "We've been on the trail for a month and a half?"

"Where'd you folks start from?" Ned asks.

"West Texas," Ollie responds.

"Six weeks. You made that crossing in six weeks. How?" Ned asks, almost demands.

"Straight across the desert," Ollie responds.

"Through Apache Territory? The desert? In the summer? Six weeks? That's a story needs to be told," Ned says, looking at the group with amazement.

"Let's just keep that story between us, Ned. Some things just need to be unspoken," Ollie asks.

"Ok, Ollie."

"You got cargo here for me?"

"Yep. All loaded up in those big wagons you like. I hand picked the mules myself. They's in the back. Mr. Stanley figured you'd want to rest a bit before you head back east. Reserved the whole top floor of the *El Toro* for you. There's a rig around back ready. Load up you gear and the driver will take you all over there. I'll take care of all of this. You need something..."

"As always, just ask Ned," Ollie finishes the sentence.

The invading army of the Ollie caravan enters the lobby of the finest hotel in Los Angles, *El Toro*. Along with Ollie's Army comes trail dust, torn clothes, sweat stained hats and the aroma of six weeks on the trail.

"I believe we have reservations," Ollie says to the clerk.

The front desk clerk is looking down at his ledger and has not seen the gentlemen standing across the desk from him. He looks up and then further up. "You must be Mr. Stanley's guests. Mr. Von Derr's party."

"Yes... I am.." Ollie starts.

"Ollie, where in the world have you been hiding. Ain't seen you on the trail. You!" The man points at Ocher, "Please, leave my cap alone, just got it broke in," he laughs.

"What's he talking about?" Stacey asks.

"Let me introduce myself. I am Bartholomew McClean. Please call me Bart. All my friends do."

"Bart," Stacey answers.

"Some time back I made a miscalculation of manners and apparently riled that young man standing beside you."

"My husband, Ocher Jones. I am Stacey."

"You, sir, are a lucky man," Bart continues, looking at Ocher. "Mr. Jones and I had a brief discussion on the matter. A discussion he won. My cap, at the time, ended up in a pile of mule muffins. Ollie there retrieved my cap and placed it back on my head."

"Oh, Bart, that sounds awful," Stacey laughs.

"Yes, Miss Stacey, it was. However, my bald spot improved so I have the young man to thank for that. And of course, Ollie."

"Bart, you do have the gift of gab," Ollie says. "Are you here on a southern delivery?"

"Yes, my big friend. Since you left, my business has picked up. I take it, since you sold your place in Frisco, that you are relocating?"

"Yep. West Texas. Don't care for the travel much anymore. Marta don't care for it either."

"Ollie, my friend. We spent many a night on the trail. Whatever you need, please just ask."

"Bartholomew, I will."

Bart tips his hat and heads out the front door.

Ollie turns to Ocher, "You made a good friend in that man, Ocher. He means it, whatever you need, ask," Ollie says, turning back to the clerk.

On the desk are a pile of keys. The clerk separates the keys, "These two are for suites, bedroom and sitting room. The rest are just rooms with beds. You have the whole top floor."

Ollie starts to parse out the keys. "Well, Miss Austin, you get a room all to yourself as do you Mr. Vernon. Enjoy."

"Is there a place acceptable for young ladies to take a hot bath?" Stacey asks.

"Two doors down, there's a ladies parlor," the clerk answers. "Across the street from the salon is a bath house, for the men."

"Mr. Jones, please avail yourself of the bath house. And take them along with you," Stacey looks toward the rest of the assembly. Miss Austin and I will see you at seven, for supper. Please dress appropriately."

"Yes, Mrs. Jones. And I will take care of our traveling necessities," Ocher says as Stacey and Austin walk out the front door hand in hand.

Apparently Stacey and Austin had contrived a plan even before leaving Texas concerning 'appropriate dress.'

When Ocher returns from the bath house, his 'appropriate dress' clothes are lying in one of the chairs in the sitting room. On top of the clothing is a note.

We will meet you downstairs in the dining room.

Ocher can hear the rustling of clothing in the next room, behind a closed door. So, as directed, he dresses and goes to the dining room to await Mrs. Jones.

Already assembled are the rest of the male contingent, also attired in 'appropriate dress.'

There is only one empty table in the dining room. The place is full. Ocher and company are escorted to a large, reserved corner table. The noise in the room is akin to cattle mewing around and grazing. The only real difference is the occasional raucous laugh.

Ocher is about to sit down when all conversation in the room ceases. The male contingent looks toward the dining room entranceway. There, taking all of the oxygen out of the room, are two of the most beautiful women ever to grace the dining room in the *El Toro*. Stacey and Austin.

Ocher is speechless, but so is everybody else in the room. The maître de escorts the two ladies to the table. Every eye in the place follows them.

"Gentlemen, please be seated," Stacey offers.

Ocher hips the maître de out of the way and holds out the chair for Stacey. Vernon figures out that he should do the same.

Ocher recalls Bart's statement *'You are a lucky man.' Don't I know it,* he thinks.

Vernon doesn't know what to say. Finally he stammers, "Austin."

"Adorabella, for this evening. My given name," Austin says.

"Ok," is all Vernon can think of.

Slowly the mewing of the other customers starts back up.

Both ladies are dressed in pale blue gowns, hair coiffed, rouge applied and painted fingernails, not a sweat stain showing anywhere.

The menus are presented, but Vernon can't do much more than to stare at Austin. He's not the only one.

Supper is ordered and served.

Vernon finally works up the courage, "Where did Austin come from?"

The Petersons found our wagon just outside Austin. My mom and dad died of consumption, so the Petersons just took me along with them. Adorabella, just a proper name, I'm still just Austin."

"No you ain't, Adorabella. You sure ain't," Vernon states.

After weeks of beans and beef with biscuits, the food at the *El Toro* is divine, plus all topped off with peach cobbler.

Ollie pushes back from the table, "I need to walk a little of this off. Anybody up for a stroll?"

The whole gang agree and take to the street, taking note of the stores and shops as they stroll about. Stacey makes mental notes about where she's going to take Austin. Tired, full and sleepy, they return to the hotel and call it an evening.

About two hours later there's a knock on Ocher's and Stacey's door. Ocher opens the door and there stands Austin, bedroll in hand.

"I'm sorry, Uncle Ocher, but I ain't used to sleeping alone in a room. The bed's too soft. Can I bunk on the floor over there?"

"Sure, Austin. Over there would be fine."

Before Ocher can close the door Vernon is standing there bedroll in hand.

"Over there, opposite Austin," he points.

Being used to trail time, well before dawn, the whole tribe is in the dining room having coffee waiting for breakfast when the sun comes up. Bart is waiting for them.

"Ollie, my friend, I'm hearing some things," Bart says, pouring coffee into his cup.

"Go ahead, tell us all."

"Folks are mighty curious how you come across the desert. Well, your gear and you all don't look done in. That's one thing. The other is, well, Ollie everybody knows you. Kind of hard to miss. They know you sold the place up north and your stuff is here. There's some around figuring that since your belongings are here so is the money for your place. Big as you are, there's some saying it's easy pickings."

"Thanks, Bart. We'll watch our back trail. We're all pretty trail wise," Ollie responds.

"I wouldn't want to tangle with this bunch. I already know about that one," Bart says pointing at Ocher. "It's still a mystery how you came through Apache Territory."

"Keep this to yourself, Bart. But Ocher, there is blood brother to Geronimo," Ollie answers.

Bart sits back in his chair, "Seems to me you was traveling with a Crow when we met."

"Ojos. Spent the summer up in Utah with him and his wife," Ocher states.

"Wait a minute," Bart starts. "There's a story going around on the docks about a kidnapping of a girl by some assassin group. She poisoned them and escaped. That wouldn't be you, would it?" Bart looks at Stacey.

"I had help, a lot of help," she answers.

"Mercy. I kind of feel bad for any of those sluggards who may consider coming at you. But not too bad," Brad continues. He looks at Ollie, "Ollie, you got friends about. Watch yourself. I know these are tough people, still, keep them safe. I'll be here abouts for a couple of days," Brad says, as he gets up from his chair.

"You stay safe as well, and thanks," Ollie says, stands and offers his hand.

Chapter Thirty-Three

The next several days, shopping, business, banking and more shopping fill the daylight hours. The evenings, well, Mrs. Stacey Jones and Adorabella Von Derr captivate the dining room of the *El Toro*.

"I hope there's room in the wagons for all of those clothes you two been buying," Ollie says, one evening over roast pork loin.

"We do, Mr. Von Derr. I checked," Stacey smiles as she responds.

"Good, you two sure do look mighty fine in those gowns and such," Ollie continues. "Be a shame not to charm all of west Texas."

"Can we..." Adorabella begins.

"Of course we can," Ocher says as he pushes back from the table. "We'll take our walk and then stop by for that ice cream, like we have every night we've been here. Get your fill. There ain't none back home. Not yet at least."

After letting Vernon recover from an ice cream headache, the whole crew decide to head back to the *El Toro*.

"You all go ahead. I'll pay the bill and catch up," Ocher says. The gang step out of the shop and turn right toward the hotel. As soon as they are out of sight, Ocher approaches the owner. "I see you or one of the other folks turning those machines to make the ice cream. Is it possible to buy one of those things?"

"Well, mister, we keep a couple of extras in the back. They're made by the Johnson Ice Cream Freezer Co. back east. Where you figuring on making ice cream? Nothing personal but competition I don't need."

"No need to worry. West Texas shouldn't worry you none."

"Well, ok. I reckon you don't want to tote that thing around. Where should I deliver it?"

"Stanley Shipping warehouse."

"I'll see that it gets to Ned first thing in the morning."

"Thanks." Ocher pays for the ice cream and the Johnson Ice Cream Freezer and steps out of the shop. Ollie and the rest of the party have disappeared. He knows they turned right toward the hotel and should be visible and close enough for him to catch up, but they are nowhere in sight.

"They're in the alley a couple of blocks ahead of you," Bart says, running across the street toward Ocher. "Six men, some with pistols, forced them into the alley. I couldn't stop them and I saw you through the window there. I've sent for some teamsters, friends of Ollie's."

"Ok. Do you know if that alley is a dead end or not?"

"No, it's not.

"When your friends get here have them go around back and cut off that escape route. I'm going in from this side."

"Just you?"

"Ollie and a whole bunch of trail wise folks are in there. Once we cut off the alley we'll have the advantage. Guns or no guns."

"Ok. Good luck."

Ocher proceeds to the alley and steps into the opening so that he can see the situation and he can be seen. *Have to stall until the other end of the alley is covered*, he thinks.

"Those are friends of mine," he says, as he steps into the opening of the alley. "Let them go and you won't get hurt."

"Us get hurt?" the comment comes from a small, dirty faced man holding a gun pointed in the general direction of Ocher. "Got it backward, mister. Now, we want you to empty your pockets and purses. One at a time, beginning with you mister." The small man continues pointing toward Ocher.

"No. As I said, leave them alone and get out before you get hurt." Ocher notes two things. One: There's a man behind Austin with his arm around her throat in a choke hold. Two: Bart just peeked around the corner of the other end of the alley and smiled.

"What do you mean, no. Empty them pockets mister or I'll shoot to kill." The man aims the pistol straight at Ocher.

"Last chance," Ocher replies.

"Yep, yours," challenges the small man.

During the verbal exchange, Ocher notes that Stacey is standing next to Austin unguarded. Apparently the robber thinks he can control Stacey by controlling Austin. Stacey slips a boot knife to Austin.

Ocher nods.

Austin drives the boot knife into the man's right leg. He screams and lets go of her.

Ollie is guarded by two men. They're facing Ollie, each brandishing a knife. At the scream they look toward Austin. Ollie reaches out and grabs each man by the throat, one in the left hand the other in the right, lifts them off the ground and tightens the grip. The knives are dropped to the ground.

Butch is guarded by one man and pinned against the building by the man's hand on his chest. Again, the man reacts at the scream. So does Butch, with a right cross to his guard's chin.

The man watching Vernon and Jimmy decides that he and his associates have lost control and heads for the rear of the alley, right into Bart and his men.

Ocher takes a quick step forward as the small man with the gun looks over toward the scream. Ocher reaches out and takes the gun and steps back. "Now what? You should have listened."

Austin is moving toward Vernon. The man with the knife in his thigh has removed the knife and is coming after Austin. Vernon sees the man and advances toward the man to protect Austin.

Ocher sees all of this, plus, he's facing the small man who has pulled a large skinning knife, apparently thinking of using it on Ocher.

Ollie is right handed, so he throws the man he's holding in his right hand at the man pursuing Austin.

Ocher sees that Austin is safe so he turns his attention of the man with the skinning knife. He gives the man the come ahead hand gesture. The small man advances. So does Ocher. The small man lunges. Ocher just swats the knife hand aside, steps in and head butts the man. All six attackers are neutralized.

"What's going on here?" comes the question at the entrance of the alley.

Ocher turns to see two men holding drawn guns, law enforcement badges shining in the moonlight.

Ocher's crew, Bart's crew and the law enforcement contingent all gather back at the ice cream parlor.

Bart's rough and tumble teamsters are used to the elements, robbers and in all cases just plain tough. There they are, all sitting around with tiny spoons held in weathered hands eating ice cream out of crystal glasses, smiling and joking.

Statements are taken. The attackers are known to the deputies and are immediately marched off to jail while Ocher and company are escorted back to the hotel.

Chapter Thirty-Four

Around the camp fire after ten days on the trail, Austin says, "Know what I miss most about Los Angles?"

"Ice cream," comes the reply from almost everybody."

"Ok, ok. I do miss it."

Ocher remains silent. He has the freezer hidden in the wagon and is still trying to figure out the ice part.

The trip east has been reasonably uneventful. Just desert, heat and mules. The Pinto wanders about during the day and stays in the camp at night.

The trail markers make the trip almost bearable.

Ocher rides up alongside the lead wagon on the Pinto. "Ollie my friend, I'd rather have the quiet boredom of the last two weeks than have to deal with whatever fracas is causing those gun shots."

Ollie stops the lead wagon. "Don't sound one sided does it? What do you think, Ocher?"

"Well, I think we can rule out Indians. This is Apache Territory. They ain't fussing with each other. They sure wouldn't let the Army Lieutenant corner them. The Arapahos are well north of here. The Comanches are well south."

"Comancheros?" Ollie offers.

"Could be," Ocher responds. "Let's move up to that rise ahead. Keep the wagons in the bottom and you and me go take a peek."

"Ok."

The caravan moves forward about half a mile, stops, and takes a defensive position. With those in the camp locked and loaded, Ollie and Ocher climb to the ridge.

Below them, trapped out in the open, is Troop B under the command of Lieutenant Dexter Ambrose. They are in big trouble. About thirty Comancheros have them pinned down and are systematically eliminating Troop B. Dexter is hiding under a wagon apparently having abandoning his obligation of command.

"How we gonna handle this, Ocher?" Ollie asks shaking his head.

"We hold the high ground from here. If we get everybody up here we can get them in a cross fire. Maybe we can run them off. Can't just do nothing," Ocher responds. "Either way, we'll have to deal with the Comancheros later on. Might as well be now."

"I'll get everybody up here," Ollie says, pushing himself down below the rise.

Ocher gives instructions to those assembled along the ridge. "When I give the signal open fire. Then stagger your shots so they won't know how many are up here. Ollie and I will be over there on the end so they can't get around the point of the rise and outflank us."

Ocher raises his hand and then drops it. Six rifles open up and six men go down. All heads turn to the ridge. Someone in Troop B, not Dexter who is still under the wagon, comprehends the action. Troop B takes offensive action and opens fire. The Comancheros are now confused. Several riders charge the hill, but don't get very far. A small group do try and come around the point but are stopped. Troop B is advancing on foot.

Over the gun fire, Ocher hears a cry of pain from the ridge. He can't stop and determine who.

The Comancheros rally and start a charge against Troop B but stop. What's left of the attacking party turn and race away.

"Cease fire," Ocher says as he stands. "Somebody got hit."

Ollie stands, "Yea, I heard." He looks across the valley at the war party of Apaches chasing the Comancheros.

Austin is kneeling alongside a bleeding Vernon.

Ocher kneels down next to Austin and cuts away Vernon's shirt. There's a through and through bullet wound just above the right collar bone. "Let's get him down to the wagon."

Butch and Jimmy lift Vernon and start toward the wagons. "Ollie, I'm going over the rise down to the Army. Meet you all there."

"Ok."

Ocher approaches Troop B and sees several dead and wounded. Dexter Ambrose is lying just beyond the wagon in the dirt bleeding from his head.

"Man are we glad you came along. Thanks. I'm Corporal Hightower," he holds out his hand.

"Ocher Jones, Corporal. He ok?" Ocher points toward the Lieutenant.

"Him. He tripped over the wagon tongue as he crawled out. He'll live. We got men who need more attention than he does."

Ocher nods, "We got one wounded but they should be here soon."

Ocher and the Corporal walk through the camp checking the wounded and identifying the dead. By the time Ollie and the wagons arrive the most seriously wounded are being treated.

Dexter Ambrose regains consciousness at the same time as the wagons arrive. He demands immediate treatment.

Stacey steps down from the wagon, looks around ending her assessment on Dexter. "Shut up, Lieutenant. We'll get to you when we take care of those that need it." She turns and joins the rest of her wagon train companions to start treating the wounded. Even Vernon, his arm in a sling, is helping the wounded, and as has become the custom, under the watchful eye of Austin.

Finally Ocher walks over to a very agitated Lieutenant. "Let me see that bump on your head, Dexter." Ocher says, pointing toward the bloody bandage.

"A bullet grazed me while we was holding off that savage attack by the Apaches," Dexter Ambrose exclaims.

"Dexter, we saw the whole thing. That is not a bullet wound. You tripped over the tongue of the wagon after you crawled out of your hiding place. And you were not attacked by Apaches," Ocher comments as he cleans the blood off Dexter's head.

"Sir, are you disputing the fact that we were attacked by Apaches led by Geronimo himself?" Dexter huffs.

"Lieutenant, you've been leading this troop around out here advertising the fact that you have no business out here. Those were Comancheros that attacked you. If we hadn't come along they would have killed you all and picked the camp clean of anything and everything," Ocher starts.

"Those were Apaches," Dexter continues to try and sell his ruse.

"Dexter, just use your head. Hear that shooting off in the distance. That's the savage

Apaches chasing the Comancheros. You don't really believe Apaches would shoot other Apaches, do you?"

"No telling. They are savages."

"We'll camp with you tonight, bury the dead and treat the wounded. Tomorrow, well tomorrow you should take what's left of your command and head back to Oklahoma. You won't be bothered," Ocher says, as he turns and walks away.

"I saw that Apache Chief Geronimo leading that attack," Dexter exclaims at Ocher's back.

Ocher stops, turns casually, "Geronimo is the medicine man for the Apache Nation. He does not lead attacks. He is no where near here. You do not concern him in the least. Dexter, go home."

"My orders..."

"Your orders were not to bring ninety men out here and return with twenty. Look around man, you have roughly ten men who are barely able. You have little or no supplies, odds are you have no idea where you are or how to get out of here. You have wounded. Go home, try and explain to the Regiment Commander how this happened. Those were Apaches that chased off the Comancheros. If they wanted you dead, they would have just stayed over that rise and let you be killed. Go home."

"Hightower!" Ocher raises his voice and shouts.

"Yes, sir."

"Make camp. No need for sentries. Have someone take stock of your supplies."

"Yes, sir."

"Butch, Jimmy, with all of that commotion south of here, maybe some deer or other game is moving north. See if you can bring in something to feed these men."

"Yes, Uncle Ocher."

By sunset there are two deer roasting over camp fires. The wounded have been treated with only one additional death. Lieutenant Ambrose sits by himself. Corporal Hightower reports the condition of the Troop to him.

Hightower walks over to Ocher who is sitting with Stacey, Austin and the recovering Vernon. "Ocher, sir.."

"Just Ocher, Corporal."

"It's Eugene, Ocher. The men call me Gene."

"Ok, Gene."

"You keep calling those men Comancheros. Who are they?"

Ollie walks over after hearing the question.

"Ok if I answer that Ocher?"

"Sure."

"Well, they started off as traders. Trading with the Indians out here. Trading in all kinds of goods. The Comanches seemed to be their best customers. The goods they wanted were guns and gun powder. During the war those things became hard to come by, legally. So they started stealing them, from everywhere. Stealing seemed to be the most profitable means of attaining guns and other goods so they just kept doing it. Now they are just plain bandits and scavengers."

"Oh," Hightower responds.

"They would have kept you pinned down until every last one of you was dead. Then they would have come into camp and taken everything. Including the clothes you are wearing."

"Oh," Hightower says again.

"The Apaches are warriors. They have a warriors creed. The Comancheros have no creed," Ocher adds.

"Will they come back?" Hightower asks.

"Not that bunch," Ocher responds. "The Apache hunting party that was nearby ran them down and killed them, most likely."

"Won't the Apaches kill us?" Hightower asks.

"No reason to," Ocher continues. "One troop of ill equipped, poorly trained and incompetently led gaggle of men wandering about in the desert is no threat to the Apache."

"We are all veterans of combat. But not this. You are correct about some of the things you said. We are not prepared for this type of war, if it comes to that," Hightower says, avoiding saying anything that the Lieutenant might take exception to.

Ocher looks up into the sky, "See that bright star there?" he points. "That's the direction you

should head to get back to Oklahoma. Aim the
tongue of the wagon at that star each night you
camp. Each morning take a compass bearing
from the tongue and follow that. It will lead you
straight back to familiar territory."

"I'll pass that along to him," Hightower says,
pointing to the Lieutenant.

The next morning Hightower is moving
about the Troop's encampment making ready to
depart. He accepts a cup of coffee from Ocher.

"I spoke to the Lieutenant this morning and
told him we were heading home. He just
nodded. I'll put him in the wagon and hopefully
he snaps out of this. Ocher, thanks. Tell your
friends out there thanks as well. I believe most of
us have had our fill of this place and them. I'm
going to take up farming. The rest I don't know."

"Gene, you watch yourself. The Apaches
won't be a problem. He will," Ocher points
toward the Lieutenant. "That man will accuse
you of taking over his command and any other
thing he can think of to save his career." Ocher
hands Eugene Hightower a piece of paper.
"That's where we all will be. You need us to
testify or you need anything, you just send for
us."

"You think he would do that?"

Hightower hears several people say, "Yes."

Chapter Thirty-Five

The remaining three weeks go by as easily as boredom, heat, and monotony can be endured. The trail markers relieve the caravan from stopping and hunting for water or food. It's just a long and hard on the butt journey.

"Riders coming in, Ollie," Ocher says, just as the sun appears.

Ollie ambles over to Ocher's side, "Looks like your Apache friends."

"Sure is," Ocher replies. "That's Geronimo in the lead."

The small party of a dozen braves arrive and spread out behind Geronimo.

"*Nd'e' Sdzan*," Geronimo grunts and smiles.

"Welcome, my friend. Please join us at the fire. There is coffee or spring water for all," Ocher offers.

Geronimo dismounts and walks, without making a sound, up to Ocher, "The Pony Soldiers have gone."

"Yes," is Ocher's only response.

"They have learned little of the desert. They will be back," Geronimo says, looking straight at Ocher.

"Yes," Ocher repeats.

"My brother, the leader of the Pony Soldiers is full of hate for you. You have placed much disgrace on his lodge. He will not forget."

"Yes," Ocher murmurs.

"He has many friends in his camp. Beware."

"You as well, my friend. His hate is for both of our camps," Ocher says, looking straight at Geronimo.

"Yes," Geronimo replies. He turns, looking back at Stacey. "The morning sickness is upon you. She will be welcome in all Apache camps." He smiles again and walks away.

"What did he mean by that?" Ocher asks.

Ollie just laughs.

Austin just shakes her head, "Men. I'm gonna be an Aunt."

Contact information:

Mike Gipson

msguscg@gmail.com

If you enjoy any of the books in this series, I would appreciate a posted review on Amazon.
To all my friends and readers, Thank You for your continued encouragement.

Made in the USA
Middletown, DE
29 June 2020